Kate le Vann was born in Doncaster and lives in London. She has written for newspapers and magazines, including *CosmoGIRL!*, *Vogue*, *Company* and *The Big Issue*, and is the author of two novels for adults, *Trailers* and *Bad Timing*, published by Viking Press, and two highly acclaimed novels for teenagers, *Tessa in Love* and *Things I Know About Love*.

Praise for *Tessa in Love*

The developing attraction . . . is handled with a rare grace and ranks as one of the finest evocations of young love that I have ever read – subtle, delicate and utterly moving.

Jan Mark, *Books for Keeps*

Had me living with the characters, laughing with them, changing the world with them, and if I dare admit it, crying with them. A fabulous story – I couldn't put it down.

Wendy Cooling

It is impossible not to feel for Tessa and her friends because they are not just photo-romance puppets but lively, serious intelligent and committed; people anyone would want to know, anyone would love.

Carousel

Praise for *Things I Know About Love*

Compelling, poignant and uplifting in the most unusual way, Kate's writing is perfectly pitched.

Claudia Mody, bookseller

KATE LE VANN

Two Friends, One Summer

Piccadilly Press • London

Text copyright © Kate le Vann, 2007

A catalogue record for this book is available
from the British Library

ISBN-13: 978 1 85340 914 1 (trade paperback)

3 5 7 9 10 8 6 4 2

Printed in the UK by CPI Bookmarque, Croydon, CR0 4TD
Cover design by Simon Davis

Papers used by Piccadilly Press are produced from forests grown
and managed as a renewable resource, and which conform to the
requirements of recognised forestry accreditation schemes.

Chapter 1

You just know when you've drawn the short straw. The bad luck clouds gather overhead and you can feel the weight of doom settling on your shoulders. I'm there, smiling hopefully as if looking cheerful might make a difference, silently praying my hunch is wrong . . . but, well, I could already tell who was taking me home with them. I just knew.

We've arrived at Vernon station in Normandy, me and my best friend Rachel, and there's two cars waiting for us. One is this gorgeous white open-top Italian sports car, and leaning against it, with her legs crossed at the ankles, is a stunning-looking older woman in sunglasses and a girl my age who might have just stepped out of a perfume ad, both of them smiling. The other car is this bashed up Citroën painted two different shades of blue, with rust around the wheels, and a short, fat man glaring out the window at me from the driver's seat. The stunning woman strides forward with her arms out to both of us, and says (like there was ever any doubt about it), 'Ray-shell?'

Rachel and I managed to talk our parents into sending us on an educational French holiday. A bit like an exchange, but one-way, for people who've left it too late for the whole exchange thing but want an intense French crammer course before their exams: this was the last summer before our final A-level year. I found the agency on the internet after a journalist my mum always reads had written about her daughter going with them the year before, so Mum was convinced they could be trusted. It was my idea, but better French wasn't really the main reason for going. I just thought Rachel and I would have a blast. We'd get our first taste of independence and frogs' legs while falling in love with beautiful French boys with sexy accents.

This is hard to believe, but it was easier to persuade Rachel's mum that it was a good idea than it was to sell it to Rachel. Anything educational is fine by her mum – she's always put loads of pressure on Rachel to be academically brilliant. Rachel's social life sometimes suffered so she could live up to her mum's expectations, and she was a bit of a late starter in the having fun business. For most of the time I'd known her, she'd been the one who stayed in doing homework or went out to orchestra practice while I necked with boys behind the chip shop.

'I don't know, Sam, couldn't it be dangerous?' Rachel asked, when I first revealed the France plan to her.

'How is it dangerous?' I asked her.

'We barely speak the language.'

'We'll get better, that's the point.'

'We could get lost or killed before that happens.'

I frowned at her, incredulous. 'How?'

'I don't know. But it's abroad. People get killed abroad. We won't know anyone. We'll be all alone. How is that better than staying at home with our friends?'

I reminded her that after six years of hanging out with exactly the same boys every day at school, we had snogged everyone we were ever going to snog there. Well, for Rachel, that was just Ginger Brian, who played the tuba in the school orchestra. Even that was quite on and off and only lasted two weeks, at which point the pair of them had spent so much of their time together blushing, they'd just about run out of blood. But my, er, more *comprehensive* snogging history hadn't brought me any closer to any love–of–my–life types. We both knew the locals weren't going to play the romantic leads in our future, or even our summer. We needed a change of scene.

* * *

3

Vernon station. Beautiful French woman throws Rachel's scruffy green rucksack into the back seat, where beautiful French girl has thrown herself. Rachel sends me a sympathetic, worried look and lowers herself anxiously into the sumptuous caramel leather passenger seat. Then her car purrs away and I'm left in the car park with the glaring old man, who finally does get out of his car only to grumpily shrug and grunt, and is now opening his boot for me to put my bag inside. He only speaks to me in French and doesn't smile *ever*. I glance into the boot, which is already nearly full with the following items: two pairs of worn out old man shoes, a big, manky toy tiger (what is that for?), a tartan rug, and what looks like a month's supply of long-life blancmanges in plastic tubs (well hey, what's weird about that? Who doesn't travel with those?). On the floor in front of my passenger seat is a pink see- through plastic (oh, please, no, in the name of all that is decent, NO!) dental plate with two false teeth attached to it. I try to sneak a glance at my driver to see if it belongs in his mouth, while carefully keeping my feet well out of its way. The bad luck clouds have finished gathering, and it's started to rain.

That was how our summer began. It makes me sound *horrible* saying this, but I couldn't help feeling that things should have been the other way around. Not because I wished toothy-blancmangey-tigery-rusty-car man on Rachel, but because I wouldn't have been as intimidated by the trendy family as she seemed to be, and, well, maybe I'd have appreciated them more. It was a bad start, but I was in France for a month with my best friend, and I wasn't about to let the first little hiccup spoil my mood. Think about it: how appealing would *my* dad be to a French girl if he picked her up from the local train station? And Monsieur Faye – my driver – wasn't the only person I'd be staying with. Rachel and I knew we'd each been put with a family with a girl about our age: mine was called Chantal. I hoped we'd get on. I'd brought her a present – a really dainty crystal-blingy watch with a pink silk strap that fastened with a press stud behind a little bow, so it looked kind of like boudoir jewellery.

Having found the Fayes' address on a map, I knew it wasn't very far from Vernon station, just outside a little town called Giverny. It was famous for being the home of the artist Monet; his house and gardens, where he did all those pictures of ponds and lily pads, were still there, and the fields around me now looked like fields he'd painted. The roads kept getting narrower the further we went, until we were driving on what seemed to be some skinny footpath down the side of a field, so the wheat on the field side brushed the car as we drove past and the low branches of the trees that stretched over on the other side tapped on the top.

Yes, it *did* occur to me that this was just some French bloke who'd happened to be in the car park at the wrong time, had started talking to Rachel's French family, and had taken advantage of the real Faye family's lateness to abduct and kill me, perhaps inserting the two teeth when the time came to eat my dead body. But Monsieur Faye had introduced himself with the right name, and seemed as unhappy about having to drive me as I was about having to be driven by him. He didn't say anything else as we drove, just twiddled with the radio and tutted when rabbits ran across the road in front of the car. I turned to look out the window at the stunning countryside, the vivid blue sky over poppy fields and distant farmhouses, and tried to guess which one I'd be staying in. Just a few minutes later, we were there.

'*Voila*,' Monsieur Faye said, and scratched his armpit.

Their house was actually a very pretty cottage, in a cluster of little stone cottages that I wouldn't have any idea about the age of – but *old* looking, anyway. Madame Faye opened the door just as I approached it with my rucksack. She had her hair in a high, tight knot and although she smiled toothily and trilled '*Bienvenue!*' in a high, loud voice, she looked unmistakably disappointed to see me, as if she'd ordered a nice sensible jumper from a catalogue and it had turned up being the wrong size and the wrong colour. And a pair of hot pants.

There was no sign of Chantal at this point, and Madame showed me to my room, insisting we spoke '*en français! Tu vas faire mieux, eh?!*', then around the rest of the cottage, talking too quickly for me to understand everything, although when she started counting things on her fingers, I could tell they were house rules. I stared at her blankly, and she sighed and repeated herself in English.

'You must not be out later than eight o'clock without you let me know where you are. We are expecting you for dinner every eve-er-ning, I demand a reason if you are not there for dinner. You can go out if you wish! But you must tell me! If you are meeting your friend, you want to spend the eve-er-ning with your friend, you tell me *en avance!*'

'Yes, *oui, bien sûr*,' I said. 'Of course I will.'

There were a lot of rules – about the bathroom and when I could use it, the kitchen and what I was allowed to eat out of it. I nodded to everything, whether I understood or not. Then she left me alone in my bedroom to settle in, and I lay down on the hard little bed, staring at the beams in the ceiling. There were grey cobwebs in the corners and I could see a couple of spiders. Like all sane people, I'm afraid of spiders, but there was nothing I could do, no one to call to get rid of them, and at least they didn't seem to be moving. I could hear the muffled conversation Monsieur and Madame Faye were having downstairs. This was all quite depressing now. Suddenly I was alone in a foreign country; there was no easy, quick way of changing my mind about it all and going home. It didn't feel much like a holiday any more, it just felt like being in a stranger's house. I lay still because moving made the bed creak and I didn't want to remind them I was there. I was afraid of even breathing too loudly.

When I checked my mobile, there was a text from a French mobile company welcoming me, in French, to its network. Nothing from Rachel. I sent her a text:

Holy crap! Scary people here. How did you get so lucky? Or didn't you? What's your house like? What are they like? Chantal not even here, not actually sure she exists!

I waited for a few minutes for a reply. When there wasn't one, I went to the bathroom to freshen up. We'd been travelling since the very early morning – train to King's Cross, Eurostar through the chunnel, another train from Paris – and I was grungey with static-y hair and sticky-feeling hands. I faced my reflection in their mirror and felt sorry for myself.

Then I realised the loo wouldn't stop flushing.

It just kept filling. I started looking around, trying to work out which towels it would be least bad to use to mop up if the water spilled over the sides. I realised this must have been part of the long bathroom explanation I hadn't paid much attention to. Finally, I took the lid off the cistern. There was a daddy long legs perched inside that seemed to look up at me, as if saying, 'Yeah? What do you want?', or, because it was a French daddy long legs, '*Oui, alors?*'. I tried not to think about what I'd do if it made a sudden move, just reached in and pulled on a little hook thing. The water stopped running and I almost cried with relief.

When I finally opened the bathroom door, Madame Faye was standing there waiting for me to come out. She looked suspiciously around me at the loo, which was now behaving itself.

'Chantal is back,' she said in French. 'Come and say hello.'

She took me to Chantal's room, knocked once and shouted that I was there. The door was opened by a very small goth. She leaned on the door frame and looked me up and down with amused eyes but a rather sulky pout, tucking her long blue-black hair behind one ear, which was pierced about fifteen times.

'Hi,' she said. 'It is nice to meet you.' I returned the compliment and the up and down look, taking in her pointy lower-lip stud, black shorts and heavy black boots. I wondered when I should give her the pink glittery watch.

Chapter 2

But I didn't really click with Rachel straight away, either, when we first met. She joined our primary school in the final year, and was a stranger-than-usual new girl. She carried what looked to us like an old lady's shopping bag (the rest of us had all got the exact same satchel with Japanese cartoons on it, which we thought was, like, total and utter coolness in 3D with Dolby surround sound) and she wore funny glasses and a full length raincoat, belted at the waist. She looked serious. Someone said that her dad was dead.

She mostly hung out with our gang, although a few other girls tried to adopt her. I liked her. She seemed a lot more mature than my other mates – not necessarily in a good way, though: sometimes she talked like your auntie, coming out with mottos or bits of advice or whatever, that just weren't the way the rest of us talked – but then she and I would find stuff funny that no one else did in quite the same way. When that happened, we'd try to explain, but only end up finding it funnier, and our voices would get higher and higher and we'd lose it a bit and our mates would look at us as if we were completely insane. She still wasn't my best friend, or even totally one of us, at that point. It was quite a nasty thing that led to her making that jump.

Rachel had this tracksuit that she brought with her for games lessons. It was a horrible burnt-orange colour and, like with so many of her other things, it was quite old lady-ish. None of us wore tracksuits – we wore little skirts and aertex shirts – but because she was new she had no idea about the way the school worked, and why her bag was weird or her coat was wrong. Although we liked her, we giggled about the tracksuit behind her back. And – I'm still ashamed when I think about this, in fact it makes me screw my face up and want to scratch it all off – one of the reasons we giggled was because she always got these massive sweat rings under her armpits when she wore it, which showed up really badly.

Anyway, so, my thing was drawing. I had a reputation for being quite good at it and I used to do little doodles of us all on request. They were cartoony and supposed to be funny, but they weren't supposed to be mean. One week I drew a picture of our gang playing netball in my jotter. I made sure to feature my big nose and my friend Hester's frizzy hair and, obviously, Rachel in her silly tracksuit. Rachel saw it along with all my mates and laughed as much as everyone else who was in it. The picture got passed around the class a bit because it wasn't bad, but when I got my jotter back, someone, I don't know who, had drawn in sweat rings on Rachel's tracksuit and wiggly whiffy lines coming from her armpits. I wasn't happy about that at all, but I just didn't let anyone else take it away to look at it, and I suppose I forgot about it.

Cut to a month later, and Rachel and I were sharing a textbook in a geography lesson, and we had to research a question about South Africa and I remembered I'd written down something about it in my jotter a few weeks earlier. When I flicked through to find it, Rachel stopped me on the page with the games cartoon, just to have another laugh at it, and I didn't remember till it was too late that the cartoon had been mucked about with. I flicked over the page as quickly as I could and pretended I hadn't seen and hoped and hoped she hadn't. But she clammed up immediately, and for the rest of the lesson sat about as far away from me as you can get on a two-person table, and I knew she'd seen plenty. It may not sound like a really big deal, but I was genuinely mortified and felt horrible. I didn't know whether to say something, but she rushed straight out without talking to me again, and I didn't get the chance.

Geography was the last lesson, and I didn't see her before she went home. Because she didn't come and join in the usual see-you-tomorrows, and because I was the last person who'd seen her, people asked me if something was up. I didn't tell them.

When I got in, I found her home phone number in my address book, and called. She gabbled something really quickly about not being able to talk now, and then she hung up before I could say anything. I heard the receiver clatter and bounce on the phone, but she hadn't put it down right and the phone was still connected. Then I heard her crying, properly crying like a little kid . . . which I suppose we sort of were, then. I called her name and she couldn't hear me, so I cupped my hands around the receiver and shouted and shouted. I was really panicking and upset by now and crying too. Eventually she heard me shouting, picked up her phone again and answered shyly.

'Sam?' Rachel said.

'I'm still here,' I said, but I couldn't think of anything else to say.

'Oh. OK.' She went quiet too. 'Well, I'll just be hanging up properly now . . .'

'Don't go yet!' I said. 'Listen, that stupid drawing – I didn't do that . . . other stuff on it.'

She sighed. 'You know, it doesn't really make any difference who did it.'

13

'It does to me,' I said. 'Because if you believe me, there's a chance you'll speak to me again. And I don't want to lose a friend over this.'

The line stayed silent.

'It's OK,' Rachel said finally. 'It was always going to happen. You wear a tracksuit like that, a lot of people'll get jealous . . .'

We both laughed, although I could hear that her laugh was still wobbling on the edge of crying, and we were both a bit snuffly-nosed now. She said she had to go, and I changed the subject because I really wanted to keep her on the phone and didn't want her to go until I knew we were OK. Rachel was different on the phone from the way she was in school – she was relaxed, funnier, she talked more. We ended up on the phone for hours, opening up about all our stupidest anxieties, feeling the importance of us both being only children, and by the end of the conversation, everything felt fixed. More than that, it sort of felt like we were both in on a secret – a good secret – and I knew already that I wouldn't talk about this to our other friends. (My mum told me off for keeping the line engaged all evening.)

It probably all seems a bit overdramatic and girly now, but friendships can be quite intense and . . . almost *romantic*, especially in the beginning, when you don't really know each other and are just like God, I *love* her! and telling everyone you know about them. Soon after

14

that, as best friends, we'd take the mickey out of ourselves mercilessly, and that day in particular, me accusing her of being hysterical, her accusing me of being evil. But I was secretly sentimental about the whole awful, embarrassing thing, because it was the first time I felt I'd had a true connection with another person.

Sometimes it's the difficult things you go through with someone that pull you together.

What I really admired about Rachel was that she never conformed, even when she could have. She could have bought the same Japanese satchel as the rest of us, or imitated the way we all talked. *I* knew – because I was her best friend – that she didn't like to bother her mum for new things. According to Rachel, her mum got pretty seriously depressed and just shut down after her dad died. Even though she was really young at the time, Rachel had to take over and get things done, and it was really hard for her. There were just the two of them in the house and Rachel said sometimes their relationship got close to imploding – I've felt tension between them every time I've been round there. They feel more like equals than me and my mum, by which I mean that Rachel always seems to spend as much time looking after her mum as the other way round. But anyway, I *know* that's not the reason she never bought into being the same as everyone else. Despite her shyness and reputation for extreme sensibleness, Rachel has never been afraid to be true to herself. When I was on a giddy/funky rollercoaster of emotions over some boy, she'd tell me what she thought, not what I wanted to hear. When I was trying to get over a life-threatening case of embarrassment because of something that had happened at school, I looked at the way she handled being teased – she met things head on and didn't pretend to feel whatever the people who were making fun wanted her to feel, just to get off lightly. I know that when I'd been bullied, however mildly, I pretended to be a good sport when I wasn't at all, or blushed and covered my face with my hair. Rachel talked back, she explained herself, sometimes she even bored people into withdrawing what had been quite offhand intimidation – that was quite cool. It's weird, because you don't really associate being brave with shyness, but they go together pretty well.

Rachel was my best friend because she was the best person I'd ever met. I'm not so sure I know why she liked me.

Chapter 3

My first morning in France. No matter how bad yesterday had been, today I was going to turn everything around and begin as I meant to go on, with a positive attitude. I woke to bright sunshine filtered through pink-rose-printed curtains and the sweet overlapping chatter of bird song. Good start. I got my spongebag and shampoo together and padded lightly to the bathroom, determined to make myself look great today. There was just one *tiny* problem. I flung open the door and . . .

'Oh my God, Sam, no way,' Rachel said, for about the tenth time. 'No way!'

As I was explaining to Rachel a few hours later, Monsieur Faye hadn't yet worked out that having a stranger in the house made it a good idea to lock the bathroom door. 'Oh no, what did you see?' Rachel braced her face for the worst. 'Was he on the toilet?'

'I honestly don't know if that would have been better,' I said.

'On the bidet?'

'He was taking a bath.' I had a violently clear flashback to Monsieur Faye's grey-furred bosoms and look of open-mouthed surprise. I rubbed my eyes with the heels of my hands to try and erase the image.

Rachel covered her mouth and giggled silently until her shoulders shook. 'No way! Couldn't you hear splashy noises from outside the door?'

'No! Argggh. Why didn't I listen for them?'

'So, you've been there less than *one day*, and you've almost flooded the loo, you've seen the father of the house naked, and your new best friend is a goth.'

'Yes, yes, yes,' I said and dropped my forehead on to the table. I was back with my best friend in a café, outside in the sunshine, and it all seemed funny, now. Now I was safe. We were in Vernon, the nearest town to my village; Rachel's French family were based here in town.

'Are you finishing that brioche?' Rachel asked me.

I opened one eye and looked up at her. 'No, I'm too traumatised to eat.'

'Can I . . .?'

'Course. I'd have thought your perfect family would have already given you a six-course breakfast with caviar and champagne cocktails,' I said, peering at Rachel through my hair.

'Well . . . actually . . . that isn't so far off what they had,' Rachel said. 'It's just that *everything* is so delicious here. This jam! I shouldn't eat it, should I? You're right, I'm fat. I'm a hog.'

'Of course you're not fat,' I said, starting off angry, but going soft, because this was a conversation we had too often and it made me sad. 'I'm just obsessing over how you've landed on your feet and I've landed in . . . well.' I had to change the subject back before Rachel got caught up in food-guilt. Rachel *had* been . . . well, fat when she was very little – I've seen pictures and apparently she got called names a lot – then she was a bit, sort of, heavy in her early teens, but now she looked good. What had once been puppy fat had turned into proper sexy Marilyn Monroe curves, but the thing about curves is that you have to believe in yourself with them, and Rachel hated hers. I was always telling her – and I really meant it – how gorgeous she was and how many people would kill to have a body like hers. But she just couldn't believe me, and she moved and held herself as if she was standing in the way of the telly during a programme that everyone in the world wanted to watch.

'But I'm a bit scared of my French people too,' Rachel said. 'Victoire and her mum are so posh and *chic*, and I'm so lumpy and English and clumsy, I do feel like they must be staring at me thinking, What is she wearing? What if she breaks our dainty French chairs?

So, you know, just because it looks like I have it easy . . .'

She stared at me solemnly, and then I burst out laughing.

'My heart bleeds, you jammy git!' I said, snatching my plate of brioche back. 'Give me that. You've got your own bathroom!'

'Well, yes.'

'No naked old men in it!'

'Mm, that is definitely an advantage . . .' We started laughing again. 'What are you going to do? Can't you come and stay with me? It's like a mansion! There's definitely enough space!'

'I *wish*! Is Victoire really nice?'

'She's lovely. Her mum's lovely. *Sorry!*'

'It's fine,' I said. 'Really. It's good that one of us is happy. And Chantal isn't *not* nice, I just think she's had me foisted on her and didn't really want to look after an English girl all summer.'

'So what did you do with her all last night?' Rachel asked.

The answer was that we had eaten a very long dinner with about three more courses than I was expecting, each one more inedible than the last. Not just because of the way they tasted, but the fact that I was more than full, less than halfway through, having eaten everything put in front of me out of politeness, but not having guessed how much was still to come. We started with slabs of this greasy pâté coated with thick yellow jelly, on slices of stale baguette. That was followed by watery brown soup, with bloated peas and bits of undissolved stock cube floating in it. Then, maybe the worst of the lot, the fish course. Guuuhh, stinky, chewy chunks of grey fish in a gluey parsley sauce, I honestly thought I wouldn't be able to swallow it. I must have been pulling a face when I was eating it. Then brown meat. I honestly couldn't tell you what kind of meat it was. Just brown. Chewier than the fish – and yes, that's what you'd *expect* from meat – but the fish had set the bar for chewiness quite high. Finally, a wet, runny crème brûlée, which wasn't brûléed, just wobbly and white all the way to the top with a bit of brown sugar sprinkled on it. *'C'est très bon,'* I said, *'mais je suis . . .'* before I realised I didn't know the word for 'full'.

'Oh Lord. Poor you,' Rachel said, mirroring my expressions as I described it. 'Our dinner last night was really nice. There was an amazing chocolate and cherry gateau, and I had three pieces – they made me! Not that I was complaining . . . Oh, sorry, um, and what about Chantal? Did you get to know her a bit? She's at school with Victoire and her friends: they said she was quite intense?'

'Well – she definitely has a sense of humour . . .'

* * *

I gave Chantal the watch, and she was obviously horrified by it, but also clearly amused. She snapped it on above her little leather knotty bracelets and nodded, assuring me it was *'charmant'*, and even I wanted to laugh, because it was so insanely wrong for her. But I didn't laugh, because I was also just mortified. Then she asked if I wanted to use the internet, and I jumped at the chance. She left me alone for about an hour in her room, which was covered with posters of bands I'd never heard of – Anomie, Abductee, loads of A-names – and photographs of her with her friends, who were also all goths or emos or whatever. I wrote some emails saying *'I want to come home, let me come home'*, then deleted them without sending because I didn't want my parents to worry, or any of our friends – who had been satisfyingly jealous of me and Rachel when we told them our holiday plans – to be able to gloat.

I went to my favourite internet talkboard – one based in America which I first found so I could talk about American telly programmes, but it was sort of bigger and friendlier than that now, more of a community – and told all of the people I knew there about it. They were really nice and said they'd still swap places with me, and that felt good. It's weird how close and supportive an internet community can feel, people you've never met giving you (((((hugs))))) they honestly mean. Then it was basically time for bed, or late enough that I could pretend it was. Chantal's parents were downstairs, Monsieur Faye laughing till he coughed at a French comedy, and I went down and told them I'd had a long day and was going to get an early night – in French – and then I went to my bedroom and tried to work out if the spiders had moved, and fell asleep at about eleven.

'Oh,' Rachel said.

'Yeah. But I was tired, anyway. I don't think I'd have been fit for much more than that. How about you?' I said. 'And why do I already know I don't really want to hear this?'

'Well, we just walked into town – Victoire's house is only about ten minutes from here – to this little bar, I can show it to you, actually it's pretty cool, and I met her friends: Marthe, Océane, and – oh, what was the other one called? They were all *totally* gorgeous, like her. I was just like . . . you know what I look like.'

I sighed. 'Anyway. I can't believe you were in a bar with people our age! I was eating slop and going to bed with spiders!'

'It was intimidating though! They're all lovely, but they're so good-looking and they talk really fast – you know I can't speak French as well as you can. Well, they did speak English a lot to me. I was just wishing you were there all night. Not because I was worried about you, although I was, but because I just needed you there, you know, but I couldn't really say, "Let's go and get my friend", and your place is quite far out, isn't it? – and I didn't know what you were doing.'

For some reason, Rachel's phone network didn't automatically switch to the French mobile provider the way mine had and she hadn't got my text. So before we split up again, we went and found a phone shop and got new French sim cards. Rachel showed me the bar she'd been to the night before.

'Did they drink alcohol?' I said.

'Yes, they shared a little jug of wine, you know – how French! – but I didn't. Victoire didn't, either.'

'Were there boys there?'

Rachel's face suddenly broke into this huge, wide, involuntary smile.

'What?' I said. 'What happened?'

'Oh, nothing,' Rachel said, seeming to snap out of it. 'They know loads of people, that's all. We were walking in the street on the way home, and it was warm, it was all new, and like, here we are in *France*, in the middle of summer, I just had this . . . *tingle* last night like we were really living, really out in the world!' Her eyes started shining again. Then she caught my gaze. 'Things are going to get better for you; we've hardly been here any time at all,' Rachel said, squeezing my hand. 'I really believe we're going

24

to have the best summer of our lives, like you promised.'

As she talked about her first night, I could picture everything – the gorgeous girls and dark, beautiful boys, people laughing and spilling on to warm streets – leaning against each other, rowdy and laid back, teasing each other the way we used to with the boys back home. I thought about the five course heavy Faye feast, the creepy crawlies everywhere and the naked man in the bath, and felt a sharp stab of loneliness, mixed with envy and homesickness – already! Sam, you wimp! – but I made my own smile bigger so Rachel wouldn't see how I felt.

It was a long walk back to the Faye house, through Giverny and along the corn fields. (Monsieur Faye had given me a lift to Vernon to meet Rachel; he hadn't looked happy about it, maybe because I'd already seen too much of him that morning. Ahem.) As I walked, my mood began to change. I kept thinking about what Rachel had said, the stuff about the 'tingle' she was getting from being here. I was angry with myself because I didn't feel the same – but the more I thought about it, being angry just seemed stupid. I was in charge of my own life in a way I hadn't been before, and that was . . . *tingleworthy*.

Things were about to get tinglier.

Closer to the little cluster of cottages where the Faye family lived, I ran into Chantal talking to a gorgeous older boy, and thought, blimey, top score, Chantal. But he looked absolutely nothing like the boys in the photographs in her room – all those pale, black-haired, pierced male versions of her. This one had sandy-brown hair and tanned, even skin, and he was wearing jeans and a tight-fitting petrol-blue T-shirt with a small v-neck. When Chantal greeted me with an unexpected smile, he turned round to face me and swept his eyes up and down my body in a way that made me want to blush. As if he didn't care whether it bothered me.

'This is my brother,' Chantal said. 'Lucas.'

'*L'anglaise?*' Lucas asked her.

'*L'anglaise,*' I confirmed.

'How do you like Giverny?' Lucas asked me.

'This is just my first day, really' I said. 'It's beautiful.'

'Her friend is staying with Victoire Lacasse,' Chantal told him, and raised one eyebrow.

'And the friend is also English?' Lucas asked.

'Yes,' Chantal nodded.

Lucas said something very quickly to his sister that I didn't understand, to which she shrugged, then he said to me, 'How long are you staying?'

'A month. Four weeks.'

I'm going to pause here, because I realise that, written

down, this doesn't look like an exciting conversation. I have to explain what's happening while this is going on: Lucas just does not take his eyes off mine! Oh my God, his eyes! Brown, with a kind of golden star around the pupil, and *steady*, maybe laughing at me, or *with* me, I have no idea, it hardly matters – and he doesn't even seem to *blink*! It's like I'm caught in a hypnotic beam, my heart rate has suddenly tripled and I'm honestly thinking, Is this what love at first sight is like? while trying to remember the second-person-present-participle of *être*. Of course Chantal is also standing there, and I'm suddenly aware that she must really now think I'm an idiot.

'What have you shown her of Giverny?' Lucas asked his sister.

'Nothing, she just got here yesterday afternoon,' Chantal reminded him. 'We ate dinner, she went to bed.'

'Exciting,' Lucas said, flashing his eyes at me again. 'Do you want to see the river? L'Epte?'

'Uh, now?' I said.

'Yes. Let's go,' Lucas said, tilting his head in the right direction.

The whole heart-pumpy thing eased off when I realised he meant me *and* his sister. But I liked watching them together: Lucas teased Chantal, but he was obviously really fond of her, and she softened up a lot with him around; she got giggly and chatty. She told me afterwards that when term was over he came back to Giverny to visit his family quite a lot, even though he had a flatshare in Paris – her eyes lit up when she said it, as if she was proud of being the reason he came home. I was thinking that, yes, maybe their parents were a bit strict, but the thing was, Rachel was making the most of our time out here straight away, getting into the freedom and new culture, while I was really being weedy and scared about being away from home for the first time. Had I even been *looking* for things to worry and complain about? So why not . . . *not* do that? We bought ice creams just before we turned back, and all the way home I had this silly big internal smile threatening to break out all over my face and make me look goofy.

Chapter 4

Chantal and I were getting on after our walk with Lucas, and she asked me along to her friends' band rehearsal in the evening. She kind of had to take me with her, I suppose, but we found a lot more to talk about on the way. Apparently, they were all taking part in a medieval summer festival in the village, with ye olde market stalls and dancing and games in the square and that sort of malarkey. This didn't seem like something a goth would be into, and I was a bit surprised by how enthusiastic she sounded, not least because she hadn't been enthusiastic about anything since I'd met her. There was something undeniably cool about her, apart from her tiny goth-ness – the way I couldn't tell whether she was laughing at me, and her slow, quiet way of talking. But as we chatted, she got quite into telling me the origins of the festival and to be honest, it was my turn to be secretly amused. She tried to explain by telling me how goths had their roots in medieval Europe, but . . . well, it was just funny having someone so dark and aloof giving me an enthusiastic history lesson.

My feet were killing me by then as I'd been walking all day, although I hadn't noticed at the time how far we'd gone with Lucas because he was so distracting and lovely. Still, for someone like me, who can go practically the whole year without stepping off concrete, it felt kind of amazing to be outside here, in the countryside, with its weird noisy calm – crickets and loud chirping birds and the sound of the wind in the trees, instead of the trafficky buzz I was used to in the middle of my home town. There were little animals running around – rabbits and mice, butterflies that were floppy and slow in the hot, yellowy sunshine at the end of the day. I couldn't believe how close we could get to the wildlife, which didn't seem at all afraid of us, as if we were all part of the same world.

The band were called Alfie, because the lead singer thought the name was cool and 'C'est punk, c'est London', and they met in the garage of a big farmhouse where one of her friends lived. I turned up expecting a hard-core indie music gig, and found even more old-school goths halfway through painting ropey chipboard scenery and sewing raggedy medieval costumes. They were also rehearsing lines for the dramatic parts, and although I didn't get the jokes because of the language, it seemed a lot like a school play. When the band started practising their numbers, they just argued with each other and the bass player would do something twangy on his own and then they'd discuss that for half an hour, then the drummer clattered through something on *his* own, all at eardrum-bursting volumes, and I didn't understand half the conversations and couldn't hear over the music the rest of the time. I was bored out of my skull. I tuned out and thought about Lucas instead, and how I finally had something good to talk to Rachel about.

'So get this, I met a boy called Lucas . . .' Rachel said.

Hang on, wasn't that supposed to be my line? Rachel had phoned to talk to me about her second night on the town with Victoire – she'd just got back in – and when she mentioned Lucas I shivered.

'Yeah?' I said, unusually nervous.

'Lucas *Faye*. And it turns out he's Chantal's brother?'

'Yeah, that's right, he just came back yesterday, we —'

'He *said* that,' Rachel said, excitedly, interrupting me. 'He's in college in Paris most of the time? I don't get it – if he was out tonight, why weren't you? Why didn't you come with him? He could have taken you home.'

The reason, I told Rachel, was because I had to go to Chantal's rehearsal.

OK, there was another reason: Lucas hadn't

31

mentioned that he was going into Vernon and hadn't asked me if I wanted to go with him. Little did I know he'd be hanging out with my best friend in Vernon while I was watching people skip around a chipboard toadstool to lute music played on electric guitars.

'He's quite flirty, isn't he?' Rachel said on the phone.

'Do you think so?' I said, feeling a bit sulky. I'd been looking forward to telling her about the *one* fun thing that had happened to me, the new sexy brother development, and it turned out she already knew about him, and had probably had a better time with him already.

'Maybe flirty isn't the right word,' Rachel said. 'But all of Victoire's friends seem to fancy him and he has that moody French thing going on.'

'They *all* have that, don't they?' I said, surprised by how argumentative I was feeling. 'It's just being French.'

Rachel laughed. 'Well that's true. But he seems a bit better at it than his friends. Didn't you fancy him then?'

'Um . . .'

'*Yes?*'

'OK, there *was* definitely a bit of flirting going on,' I said.

'Ha, I knew it!' Rachel said. 'As soon as I found out he'd met you I thought you must have made an impression. You could flirt for England.'

'Hardly,' I said quietly. The conversation was making me uneasy. The truth was, there hadn't been much flirting going on at all. I let Rachel think there was because I was embarrassed at the way our usual personalities seemed to have been switched since we'd got here. Back home the only social event she never missed was orchestra practice. Now, here I was watching the nerds of darkness rehearse their medieval – I mean, could it be sadder? – village green morris dancing, and Rachel was in the centre of town with the in-crowd, flirting with my new crush. Except he wasn't mine, and I didn't have any claim to him. I'd let the conversation go there when I talked about Lucas because I wanted to put her off him and make sure she didn't accidentally end up seducing him before I'd even had a proper conversation with him. Apart from the walk along the river, when his little *sister* was with us, and after his initial amazing, blazing stares at me, there hadn't been *any* reason for me to think he found me remotely fanciable. I wasn't used to feeling competitive with Rachel and I didn't like myself for doing it – it just came out of nowhere, this new, half-annoyed, half-anxious feeling. Even Rachel seemed foreign over here.

I got up early the next morning so I could beat Monsieur Faye to the bathroom. I said the usual *bonjour* to the daddy-long-legs in the cistern when I was stopping the loo from overflowing – I was good at that now – and tried very hard to get out of the bath without getting any water on the floor, as this was something Madame Faye had told me off for doing the morning before. I dressed and went quietly downstairs and was freaked out to discover Lucas already in the kitchen, making himself a breakfast of coffee and cold cured sausage slices on thick pieces of bread. I wasn't sure why I was so nervous around him: maybe it had something to do with lying about flirting with him to Rachel the night before, as if he'd found out what I'd said. I just wanted to turn around and go straight back to my bedroom. But Lucas had already seen me and offered me some fresh coffee.

'So I met your friend last night,' he said softly, handing me a cup.

'Rachel,' I said, also very quietly. 'Yes, she told me on the phone. Do you know Victoire?'

'Yes, lots of people in the villages went to the same school; I've known her since a long time,' he said. He was doing the steady, slow-burning stare again, and I couldn't meet his eyes – it was too early in the morning. I looked into my coffee cup instead, and blew the spiral of steam away from the top. 'Next time maybe you'll come too?'

'Well, yeah, I'd really *like* to!' I said. 'But I'm sort of, you know, supposed to stick with Chantal, to learn French, not just go around with my English friend having fun. And it was good to see Chantal's band, they're very—'

'You're not in school now, you know?' Lucas said, shrugging. 'You're not having your lessons all day. The evening is your own, you choose what you want to do.'

He popped a large piece of the bright red sausage into his mouth – croissants aside, the French eat mad stuff for breakfast – and chewed, not taking his eyes off me.

'I don't know how happy your parents would be about that,' I said. He shrugged again. I drank more coffee and, looking deep into the cup, said, 'Are you going out tonight?', trying not to sound as if I was asking him out. I peeped at him over the rim.

'No,' Lucas said, without looking at me at all, 'I'm going back to Paris today.'

What would I have given to spend the day with Lucas in Paris? Monsieur and Madame Faye had planned a trip for the rest of us to Monet's gardens, and while they were unquestionably beautiful, picturesque, blah de blah de *très* blah, there is maybe nothing on earth more boring than talking about flowers in French with middle-aged French people, while walking so slowly I thought I might actually fall over. Oh, *regardez*, there's the bridge he painted about a zillion times, there's his favourite pond. And over there, *more flowers*. Chantal was forced to come along too, and I could tell she blamed me for her Saturday being a complete bust – she'd gone back to being dark and moody, and talked in very fast French so I found it hard to keep up. I hid my yawns, she didn't. I got a text from Rachel saying she'd gone to the beach in Deauville with Victoire and co – Deauville is a really posh beach that movie stars sometimes go to, apparently – and she wished I could have gone too. I was hearing that a lot from Rachel. I'd seen her once since we'd got to France. I couldn't help feeling she'd abandoned me, even though I knew it wasn't her fault at all.

We had another long, Lucas-free Faye family meal that evening, as heavy as ever, the same tough brown meat smothered in rich sauce, despite how hot it was outside. If I went on eating like this, I was going to grow out of all the clothes I'd brought. Chantal was happy to let me use her computer again, probably because it meant she didn't have to spend all night talking to me. She sat on the other side of her bedroom watching ancient episodes of *Friends* that had been dubbed into French on a little portable telly and talking to her friends on the phone. My first Saturday night on our French adventure, and this was how I was spending it. If I'd been at home, there would have been a party, or a walk with my male and female friends watching the sunset chill to moonlight from the North Bridge, maybe a friendly snog with one of my exes. I would have done anything to teleport myself home that minute and be somewhere I belonged again.

Chapter 5

The next morning, Sunday, the Faye family went to church. There was an awkward moment when Madame Faye asked me if I wanted to come. Of course, I *didn't* want to, but I didn't know what to say. There was a silence, then she just let me off, saying there was no reason I should go if I didn't usually go. But you could tell she was thinking, Well, if you want to go to *hell*, that's fine with me . . . Chantal said I could take her push-bike if I wanted to get around a bit more easily, and I could have hugged her. I cycled into Vernon and ordered a scrummy breakfast in a little patisserie – the softest, flakiest golden pain au chocolat and a still-warm buttery croissant, with the jam that Rachel couldn't stop eating the day I'd met her in town. I hadn't called Rachel to tell her I was going to be so close to her French family's house this morning. I missed her, and I'd been missing her every day I'd been there, checking my phone for messages that didn't come. But today I felt like being alone: to comfort eat, to mope, and just to sit outside in the gentle morning sun and think, away from the Faye house. And I was embarrassed because I was always the one waiting to hear what Rachel was doing, waiting for her to say she had time to see me, then being told she hadn't. I wanted her to ask me for a change. I'd bought postcards at Monet's garden to send to my parents, although I'd been keeping them up to date by email, and some of our friends. I filled these in with more cheerful stories about the great time I was having – trying not to think too hard about how jealous they'd been of our big French plan, and how not-jealous they'd be if they knew how I was spending my days. I watched the sleepy town starting to wake up as I sipped my cup of *thé* and stuffed my face with pastry.

It did the trick. I started to relax, the tension in my head seemed to smooth out, and I felt good. Really calm and happy, as if the lies I was telling in the postcards had started to convince me. Then, some *kid*, maybe eleven or twelve years old, who'd been making his way around the tables (I'd glanced at him thinking he might start begging from the customers, and deliberately didn't look at him any more so he wouldn't approach me) grabbed my bag from the back of my chair and started running off with it. I was so shocked I just made a kind of pathetic 'uh!' sound, and before I really knew what was going on, a tall boy at another table had stood up so fast he knocked over his chair with a huge clang, and run off after the kid, so that I wondered if they were together – until he tripped the kid up, grabbed the bag off him, and tried to hold him there by clutching various pieces of the kid's clothes until they stretched out to three times their original sizes, then the kid hit the tall boy in the face, wriggled out of his grip and ran like mad, without my bag. By now I'd managed to get to my feet and make my way through the tables – excusing myself past a bunch of curious French people who were watching the show and muttering about me and my bag – and over to the boy who'd stopped the thief. He was a few years older than me. Blond. Very cute. And bleeding a little from a cut in his lip.

'Oh my God, thank you,' I said, then remembered where I was and switched to French to add, 'That's my bag.' (Duh!) 'Thank you! Are you badly hurt?'

The blond boy picked himself up and smiled shyly.

'No, of course not. I'm glad I could help,' he said, in English, although he was French. He touched his lip with the back of his hand and looked at the blood. I grabbed an unused napkin from an empty table and gave it to him.

'I'm so sorry he hit you,' I said. 'I should have been paying more attention to my stuff. Thank you so much, you really saved me.'

'He was just a child,' the boy said, shaking his head. 'It wasn't very heroic.'

We stood and looked at each other for a moment. I didn't really know what else to say.

'Oh, I'm Samantha,' I said self-consciously, and put my hand out to be shaken.

He smiled just as shyly. 'Hi, Samantha. I'm Bruno.'

That was as much conversation as we managed, and we went back to our breakfasts on separate tables, and I sort of waved, like an idiot, as I picked up my croissant again, and went back to writing my postcard. Then I had a thought.

'Oh, sorry, excuse me, Bruno?' I called over. 'I'd really like to – could I buy your breakfast, to say thanks?'

'No, really, that's fine,' he said, tilting his head to smile again. 'But thank you.' He turned back to his paper, and I saw that he had a small cup of coffee and nothing else. Wow, how flash was I, offering a reward equal to a whole euro and a half! Then I had another thought.

'I wouldn't even be able to buy my own breakfast if it weren't for you,' I said. 'So . . .' OK, enough, leave him alone, now, Sam, you total freak. 'Listen, thanks so much, this bag has got *everything* in it! My purse, my passport, my, er, sunglasses . . .'

I'm not sure how we got from this brilliant start to him joining me at my table and the pair of us ending up noisily and comically arguing about which celebrity marriages were going to last the longest – he came up with a formula which involved the couples looking the most alike ending the soonest, and I was coming up with all the exceptions – while the other French people who'd been happy to watch the bag-snatch drama unfold now occasionally looked up and glared at us for chattering constantly in loud English through their previously peaceful Sunday breakfasts. I knew I ought to be practising my French, but I was lapping up the company after having ticked off another evening listening to myself squeaking the plate with my knife and chewing gristle *chez* Faye. Also, Bruno's English was brilliant, unlike my French, making this the easiest conversation I'd had for days. He told me he was an art student, in his first year, but he was originally from round here, and came back home for all of his summer vacation because he found it the best place to sketch and paint, and it was cheaper moving back with his parents for a couple of months.

We weren't flirting or anything, by the way, just talking . . . but *really* easily. He was very different from Lucas – when I first locked eyes with Lucas it felt like electricity passing between us. Bruno was just really nice. In his own way, definitely as good-looking, but softer, quite like a cute golden Labrador, compared with Lucas's sexy Orlando Bloomy bone structure. Bruno was the kind of boy you and your friends call sweet, and you constantly ask yourselves how come he hasn't got a girlfriend, and you all sort of fancy him but the 'thing' just isn't there. 'Cause who knows why we fall for one person and not another? Sometimes I wonder if we make it hard for ourselves because if we always took the easy option, our lives would just start going too fast and we'd have to live up to them. I've always chased after boys that I couldn't get, and if I did ever somehow get them, I suddenly found all sorts of reasons to change my mind.

Anyway, I could compare and contrast different French boys all day long, but it wasn't like any of them were asking me out. All that happened was Bruno thanked me for his second cup of coffee, apologised for my having to see an ugly side to what he promised was the most beautiful part of France, and said he hoped the experience wouldn't make me worried for the rest of my stay. Then he got up and shook my hand. The French shake hands a lot.

'Well, I might bump into you again,' I said, suddenly sort of wanting to because he apparently didn't really care one way or the other. Like I said, I was always more interested in boys who weren't interested in me.

'Yes, I'm sure, it's a small town,' Bruno said, smiling. 'Perhaps we'll see your thief again, too, and we can arrest him together,' but it was obviously just a joke. As I watched him leave, I thought about all the things I could have said that might have made him stay longer or want to see me again, and realised that right now I really wanted a friend.

Chapter 6

People always say that time goes quickly when you're on holiday. I think those people are crazy. When you're spending the summer at home, whole weeks are eaten up in what feel like minutes. You throw days away just lying in bed till midday, getting up only to eat Sugar Puffs and read magazines with pictures of super-thin celebrities. Away from home, the days stretch to hold hundreds of different things, all new, and weeks go on and on without an end in sight. I didn't see Rachel again till the following Friday because the Lacasse family had taken her down south with them for a mini-break at their holiday cottage in Provence. She'd spent the time playing tennis, swimming in their private pool, and – by the looks of her – sunbathing. She and Victoire met me at a café in Vernon, and Rachel was much browner than the last time I'd seen her, her skin was gorgeously freckled, her dark blond hair wavy and pretty, and she seemed to be brimming over with energy. Victoire looked just as gorgeous as the first time I saw her, leaning against the car in Vernon station, so the pair of them were intimidatingly good-looking. I'd spent those days being dragged by Monsieur and Madame Faye around the local historical hot-spots: abbeys, cathedrals, and exciting *woods*. So much time seemed to have passed. I felt *shy*.

It could have been because I'd been looking forward to relaxing with my best friend today, but with the supercool Victoire there I was still holding back and trying to be on my best behaviour, to make her think I was cool too. Rachel was telling me about the Lacasse family's cottage in Aix, and Victoire interrupted to correct her a few times, but in that fun way, the way you want to be interrupted because it makes your story last longer, the way friends interrupt you. The way I used to interrupt Rachel.

'Anyway, how have you been getting on with Chantal?' Rachel asked, and she and Victoire glanced at each other. The look spoke volumes – it told me they'd talked about her and made fun of her – you know how you can tell these things. I'd complained to Rachel about Chantal being hard work plenty of times, but now I was surprised to find myself genuinely upset by this, as if they were insulting a close friend of mine and assuming I'd go along with it. Rachel definitely didn't mean it horribly – I think she thought I was still up for complaining about her, and that we'd have fun doing it. But the honest truth was, I *did* like Chantal now. She was as bored as I was by the educational trips her parents made us go on, but she'd stopped blaming me for them. She comically rolled her eyes when they announced their plans in the morning. Chantal and I were probably never going to be really good friends – we were too different and didn't, when it came down to it, speak the same language, in more ways than the obvious one – but I could tell that she was nice, in a gothy good-girl way.

'It's been fine,' I said, feeling a bit nervous around Victoire, so not giving much away, definitely not the evenings in with Chantal's parents playing Scrabble in French, or the progress she and her friends were making embroidering leotards for their village festival play. I didn't want them to laugh at her. 'And Lucas is sweet . . .' Remembering what Rachel had told me about all of Victoire's friends fancying him, I hoped this might quickly put a stop to them both pitying me.

'He's been in Paris, though, *non*?' Victoire said. 'I was speaking to Jean-Phillipe, his flat-mate, earlier today. Oh,' she turned to Rachel, 'Océane says we should drive there soon to go clubbing one night. Do you think that sounds like fun?'

'To *Paris*?' Rachel said. She looked at me and I saw

her eyes widen with panic. Rachel had never been into clubbing, she felt self-conscious dancing. But there was more to it than that – I think she was wondering if I would be included in the invitation. Victoire didn't address the question to me, but it would have been quite weird for her to be inviting my best friend and *not* me. Meanwhile, she had started composing a text to a friend. I felt hot and awkward so I just barged forward and changed the subject, telling Rachel about the near-robbery and about the boy who'd helped me out, and of course it turned out – well, blimey, who would have guessed? – that Victoire knew Bruno quite well too. Then her phone beeped, and she opened it up again.

'It's from Lucas,' she said. 'He says he's home this weekend, and that he'll come into Vernon now to meet us. Do we want to wait for him?' Rachel and I looked at each other, shrugging and stuttering our way through to 'yes'. I hadn't known Lucas was coming back today. Victoire texted a swift reply with her elegant French-polished fingers, and got back another text from him, which made her laugh out loud, but which she didn't share with us. I didn't think it was good that she was friends with Lucas while being snide about his little sister.

As we waited for Lucas to turn up, Victoire teased Rachel about a boy called Fabrice. I tried to follow, but it all felt like I'd tuned into my favourite TV show, and realised I'd somehow missed an episode and the plot had moved on and it was hard to catch up.

'Who's Fabrice?' I asked.

'We've only met a few times,' Rachel said. 'He came with us to the beach at Deauville that day.'

'But he likes you,' Victoire said. 'He told Marthe he thought you were pretty.'

Rachel blushed. 'I'm sure he didn't say that . . .'

'Enough, I'm texting him too,' Victoire said, grinning, and flipped open her phone again. While she was texting, Rachel grabbed at her hands and they both cracked up. I felt like an intruder, and also fairly jealous. It was like she'd taken my place. In what felt like another world, Rachel would have been blushing when I told her Ginger Brian fancied her, or trying to stop me writing a funny romantic email to GB on her computer (or, not long after that, a not-so-funny break-up email). I fixed my friend with a look that I tried to aim somewhere between finding it just as amusing as they did, and jokily telling her off for not keeping me up to date. I hoped my hurt didn't show.

'I'm sure he didn't say that,' Rachel said again to me, more quietly.

'So, um, what's he like, then, Fabrice? Anything like Ginger Brian?' This was supposed to be a joke but once it was out of my mouth I was worried it sounded snide.

47

'Nooo,' Rachel said, and fortunately didn't seem bothered. 'He's nice; I like him. I wanted to talk to you about him, but you've been so busy. And I've been so busy! It's like our French people are keeping us apart. I didn't want to send you a text about it, I wanted to talk properly. I *miss* you, I can't believe we're spending so little time together. This was supposed to be our amazing summer and we're already into the second week and I've barely seen you.' I was so relieved she'd said this so I didn't have to.

'It's the Fayes and their educational outings,' I said. 'You're allowed to do what you want, my family are taking it all too seriously and think they have to *teach* me things as part of the arrangement.'

'Plus you're so far out – you know, everyone's hanging out in town every night and you're stuck in that little village. Océane has a car, but it's always full of her friends. I don't feel like I can ask her to drive up and get you, but I really want to.'

'No, of course you can't. Honestly, don't worry about it.' I sighed. 'I just got unlucky. The Fayes have said I can go out in the evening, but Monsieur Faye has no intention of acting as my personal taxi driver and there's no other way of getting here!'

'What about Lucas?' Rachel said. 'When he's home, get him to bring you out on his moped.'

'Excuse me? Rachel "Safety first!" Chase is telling

me to get on a boy's moped!' I said. 'What's come over you?'

'It *is* safe,' Rachel said. 'You just grab on to the boy's waist as tight as you can and concentrate on not falling off. He's got a spare helmet.'

This was too much all at once.

'Seriously, *what*? When have you been on a boy's bike?' I said. 'Whose bike?'

Rachel had plucked a sachet of sugar out of the bowl on the table and started playing with it. 'Lucas's. I told you that already,' she said, concentrating on getting every grain of sugar down to one end, and then folding the paper up tightly around it.

'NO YOU DIDN'T!'

'Didn't I?' She took her concentration off the sugar packet for a moment to glance up at me.

I made an 'oh, come on!' face at her.

'Oh, well, if I didn't, it was because you were talking about there being a bit of a spark between you and I didn't want you to think I was trying to muscle in on your . . . bloke, *which I wasn't*, because as you can see I have a completely different crush.'

'What were you doing on his bike?' I asked. Victoire had stopped texting and I was aware of her listening to us, and hoped I hadn't started to look angry and crazy.

'The night we met, he just asked if I wanted to ride round the edge of town with him, and along the river,'

Rachel said. 'I thought it would be fun. Obviously I didn't know then that you were into him.'

'I'm not into him,' I said weakly. 'Well, not . . . I mean . . . I can't believe you didn't tell me.'

'It was really nothing,' Rachel said. 'I thought it would . . . *upset* you and it has, so I was right not to talk about it.'

'I just don't like not knowing,' I said. I sounded sulky, and couldn't get it out of my voice. 'Anyway, it *is* dangerous.'

Rachel smiled and turned to Victoire.

'I've always been sensible: you know, played safe, ' she said. 'Sam is just a bit shocked at how different I am here.'

'It's quite safe,' Victoire said to me, smiling kindly as if I was a little old lady. I was getting quite sick of hearing this 'Lucas should bring you when he comes into Vernon. You'll have more fun with us. We'll tell him when he gets here.'

It was now about seven p.m., and I had to phone the Fayes to say I wouldn't make it back for dinner, because that was one of their big rules. I couldn't assume I'd be eating with Rachel and Victoire, though – it was possible that it'd get to nine p.m., say, and Victoire would suddenly say, OK, we're off *chez moi* for *le dîner*, now, *au revoir*, Samantha, leaving me stranded in Vernon, hungry and alone. Victoire had an infuriating spontaneity. The thing is, I knew I'd have been exactly the same, back in England, just assuming everything was easy. But, anyway, *Lucas* was going to be here soon – so if I stuck with him I should be fine. His parents couldn't tell me off if I'd been with their son, and he could set them straight on where I'd been and assure them I was fine. Still, I had to give them notice, in case they were right now preparing enough tough brown meat for all of us. The music in the café was quite loud, so I went outside to call.

It was still daylight, but it was the time of day I liked best, where the sun felt heavy and seemed to collect in my hair and wrap me in a hug. I called, and Madame Faye answered. She told me she'd already started making dinner and then left a silence, which I duly filled with an apology in my usual patchy French. She asked me how I was getting home. I said I'd come home with Lucas.

'Lucas is with you now?' Madame Faye asked. 'He told me he'd be home for dinner. Let me speak to him, please.'

'Well, actually, he's not here yet,' I said. 'But he, er, told my friend, I mean, my friend's friend, he texted to say he was on his way.' Madame Faye didn't seem very happy with this at all.

'Of course you can stay out with your friends,' she said. 'But I need to know you have a way of getting home safely.'

I was getting stressed because I didn't know for sure that Lucas was coming, or, really, how else I might get back. I thought about how my mum would kill me if she knew that I was even considering taking risks about the way I got home in the dark, and the thought of her loving me and worrying about me, even though her over-carefulness had always driven me mad, made me want to cry. But it wasn't like my best friend was going to let me just start walking off along the corn field alone, and Madame Faye wasn't my mum, so I politely assured her that I would definitely be careful and there were lots of people ready to drop me off. She was silent for a while, then said, coldly, 'Please be home before midnight, or you will wake us.'

I hung up and theatrically rolled my eyes and said, 'Blooooody hell,' out loud, the way you sometimes do things in quite an over the top way when you're in public, alone, and think you might be being watched.

Then I realised I *was* being watched.

While I'd been concentrating on the phone call, Lucas Faye had somehow managed to park his bike outside the café, more or less exactly where I was talking, and he stood next to me now, those incredible, merciless eyes of his looking very amused.

'And how is my mother?' he said.

Chapter 7

'She's expecting you back for dinner,' I told Lucas.

He leaned against the moped, smiling mischievously. 'Well then, we'd better go back, hadn't we?' he said.

'Oh, of course,' I said, nodding, realising that I hadn't escaped another heavy dinner with the Fayes after all, and my plans to finally have a fun night out with my friend were going to be shelved again.

'I'm just joking with you,' Lucas said. 'Come on.' He opened the door to the café to let me go through ahead of him.

'Oh, but –' I said. 'Shouldn't you call her?'

'I'm not fifteen,' he said.

When we got back to Rachel and Chantal, they'd been joined by another boy, who Victoire introduced as Fabrice. Oh, *this* was Fabrice! Long black hair, skinny, big-nosed, a bit arrogant maybe, but all put together in a French way, these things were undeniably quite gorgeous. He glanced up at me without much interest, and carried on talking. He was sitting next to Rachel on the long wooden banquette, and their upper arms were pressed close together. He was smoking. Rachel didn't like smoking. Lucas pulled out a chair for me and called the waitress over, ordering a glass of red wine. It crossed my mind that he might get drunk and then I'd have to go home with him on his bike and he'd crash or take a corner badly and I'd fall off and be killed. I asked for a Coke, thinking that if I was sober it would be safer. But would I really get on a motorbike with someone if they were drunk? This was terrifying. Why was I here? OK, it was just one glass of wine, that was totally legal, totally fine, the French are used to drinking wine, calm down, Sam.

But I was really worried. It didn't feel anything like fine.

Then I saw that Rachel had a glass in front of her too.

'Is that wine?' I asked her.

'Yeah,' Rachel said, looking guilty, then, as if slightly exasperated with me, 'Just a little glass. Have some.' Seriously, when had I become the goody-goody and Rachel the racy one? I remembered a party earlier in the year when a completely sober Rachel had sat with me, talking me through a panic attack, as I flopped on the stairs with the room spinning because I'd stupidly drunk home-made punch without knowing what was in it. Of course, the next day, I had promised myself never to be so dumb again.

'Maybe in a bit,' I said, still thinking about how I'd get home. I'd been wishing so hard to be a part of this gang since I arrived in France, arrogantly telling myself over and over that it wasn't fair that Rachel had a place at the cool table, while I, *previously the cool one,* was forced to relocate to nerdville. Now I was here and couldn't find a way of belonging. I sipped my Coke and watched my best friend flirting in French. All the questions I could think of asking were lame and boring. I didn't have anything interesting to say. Half of me wished I could just give up tonight and somehow be back home with my mum watching a cheesy old movie. The other half was trying to think of ways to be more like the me back home, who had no trouble talking to people.

Some more of Victoire's friends turned up, ones I'd heard Rachel talking about: Océane and Marthe, plus more boys, until the table was stuffed with people and I didn't have to worry about not saying anything, because I knew no one was looking. At this point the conversations split, and Lucas started talking to me in English in a lower voice, asking me if I was OK, how I was getting along with his parents, and so on. We weren't really particularly clicking. I found myself pretending to smile more often than I naturally felt smiley, in case Rachel was watching me – so that the thing I'd told her, about there 'definitely' being some flirting going on between me and him, seemed true. But Rachel's attention was taken up with Fabrice, who was pressed even more closely against her since all the extra people had turned up. When we all ordered some snacks, Fabrice casually ate chips from Rachel's plate, and sometimes she glanced at me with a kind of shocked, excited look on her face. I tried to throw her back supportive looks, to let her know it was OK. Really, I needed to talk to her properly, to have a little girly time-out before things went further, but we'd be able to do that soon enough. I sent her a secret text from the loo, saying, 'Wow, you vamp! He's so into you!' and came back to see her read it and give me a huge grin.

Later, everyone lingered outside in the street, chatting before they went home. Fabrice's arm was loosely wrapped around Rachel's waist, his fingers casually drumming on her belt, and she leaned against him. My sensible friend was definitely going to get snogged tonight! I was really happy for her. But also still worried about how I was going to talk to Lucas about him giving me a lift home. This was crazy, he was going *right there*; Rachel had been on his bike just last week; it was going to be no big deal; I was just going to hop on like it was pre-planned, and we'd be back at his mum's house in ten minutes. So, OK . . .

While I was waiting for Rachel to untangle herself enough from Fabrice for me to talk to her about the next time we'd meet, I spotted a familiar face across the street: Bruno, the boy who'd rescued my bag in the café. He was walking with a couple of other boys, and when he saw me he smiled and waved, and I waved back, and I thought he was going to cross over the street and talk to me. But then he seemed to change his mind and he smiled again, a little differently, and carried on walking. I turned around to see where Rachel was and found Lucas standing next to me, also looking across the street at Bruno and his friends.

'Rachel said you would need a lift home,' Lucas said. 'I'm going now.'

'Oh, great, if that's OK?' I asked him. 'Let me just tell Rachel I'm going.'

'Of course,' Lucas said. He stood waiting for me in a moody sort of way. I could feel his eyes on me but I needed to find Rachel so I could give her a hug and tell her to be careful with Fabrice, and ask her if she was *really* sure I wasn't going to die if I got on Lucas's moped. She said I'd be fine and she'd be fine, stop worrying, and to call her as soon as I got back. I was, *again*, more than a bit freaked out that being far from home seemed to be making her worry less and me worry more.

So, that moped. They're quite cute-looking things, and they can't possibly go very fast, can they? I was thinking, as I tried to work out whether my shoes were in any danger of falling off. Lucas gave me his spare helmet and I put it on, wondering how stupid I looked. I hadn't thought to scoop all my hair back, and some of it got pushed in front of my face. My cheeks felt squished too. I stared up at him and hoped I didn't look *really* stupid.

'I've never done this before,' I said. 'What do I do?'

'Just hold on,' Lucas said.

'There's no, um, seatbelt, then?' I said, as we arranged ourselves on the seat.

Lucas laughed. 'Your arms,' he said. 'Hold me.'

But it is just so *crazy* hugging a boy you fancy and hardly know! I wanted to apologise. I worried I'd hugged too early. I worried about how tightly I should hold him . . . well, that was until he started the engine. Then I gripped him like my life depended on it. I felt the rumble of the engine under me, the wobble of the bike, and I was really scared. I had no way of stopping it or getting off. I was afraid my hands would somehow forget how to hold, or that we'd hit a bump and I'd let go and fall.

This was all before we'd left the car park.

Then . . .

As we left the town and crossed the river and zoomed through the fields, there were no street lights, no other cars, and everything around us was pitch black. I felt like I was drunk, or dreaming, or watching myself from somewhere outside me. I leaned tightly into his back, then consciously tried to sit just a little more upright and further away, daring to tilt my head to glance out at the night sky for barely a second until the dizziness made my heart almost stop with fear. Suddenly, I had a thought: what if you *stop* being scared? What if you just let it happen? I realised that my knees were gripping the sides of the bike so hard that they were almost numb. I forced myself to soften, relaxed my face, and moved my hands just *barely* so I could *feel* that I was holding Lucas's torso, and a shiver of excitement shook me so hard that I gripped just as tightly all over again.

It was a little after midnight when we got in, and the house was silent, the lights off, his parents were in bed. We bumped around in the dark feeling for lamp switches.

I wondered if he was going to stop and talk, but that didn't seem to be on the cards, maybe because he didn't want to wake up his parents, maybe he was tired, maybe he just wasn't interested in talking to me at all. We were both at the foot of the stairs, about to walk up together (to each go to our bedrooms) when Lucas stopped and turned unexpectedly so he was close enough to kiss me.

'I'll see you in the morning, Samantha,' he said. I just nodded with my mouth open, sort of idiotically. Then he turned around again and carried on up the stairs.

Chapter 8

I had a normal, awkward breakfast with the Fayes, minus Lucas, who was either still in bed or had already left. His favourite weird, dry, breakfast sausage was lying out on the table, so it was hard to tell. To my relief, Madame Faye asked me if I had any plans for the day, which usually meant she *didn't*. I lied and said I was going to meet Rachel, knowing I could always arrange that later, and I didn't want her to come up with an alternative. Monsieur Faye asked if I'd need taking into Vernon, and I thanked him but said I could walk.

After breakfast I went back to my room to call Rachel. When I'd got back the night before, I'd phoned her and gone straight to her voicemail, so I needed to find out what had happened after we'd split up. But there was a knock on my door even before I found my phone. It was Lucas. We'd just spent the evening before hanging out in a bar, like friends, but I still didn't feel relaxed around him, the way I might have if, say, someone like Bruno had just happened to be passing my bedroom and dropped in for a chat. Lucas maintained a kind of distance, as if he'd made a conscious decision not to give me any idea how he was feeling at any time.

'I'm going back to Paris today,' Lucas said. 'Do you want me to bring you somewhere before I go?'

I was gripped by a mad urge to get on his bike again. I think I'd just had too many deadly dull days one after another and last night's midnight ride had woken up a real need for *something* to happen. And OK, he'd only offered to give me a quick lift somewhere before completely forgetting I existed again, but just for a few moments this morning, I wanted to be scared and excited and going somewhere fast again. I raced around my room grabbing all the things I might need that day and stuffing them in my bag, and told him I was ready to go whenever he was. We dropped by Chantal's room; she was working on her web page and happy to send me away. She casually asked Lucas when he'd be home again, and he told her maybe next week. She shrugged and said OK, but I caught her eye when he told her *au revoir*, and noticed she looked quite sad.

Monsieur Faye had already gone to work by the

time Lucas and I got downstairs. Madame Faye asked me if I wanted to invite Rachel for dinner the following week. Right, she'll love that, I thought. But I told Madame Faye that was really kind of her, and I'd let her know with plenty of time to prepare.

I couldn't wait to get out.

My plan was just to get Lucas to drop me off in Vernon, where I could call Rachel and get her to come out and meet me, or maybe I could go round and finally see the amazing house she was staying in. She'd talked about it, but I hadn't been there.

'What time did you tell your friend you'd meet her?' Lucas asked.

'Rachel? I haven't called her to fix it up yet,' I told him, arranging my hair so the helmet would look a bit prettier this time. 'I mean she's staying almost in the centre, so I thought I'd just wander around until she can come and meet me.'

'So I could take you for a ride,' Lucas said. I grinned, wondering if he knew that had a double meaning in English.

'Well, if you have time,' I said. 'I know you have to get back to Paris today.'

'Paris is not much more than an hour away,' Lucas said. 'It's early. I'll bring you to Gaillard; it's one of my favourite places.'

'Sure,' I said, a bit confused by the offer. 'Great.'

Today, I noticed that his moped really *didn't* go all that fast, and that nerves and the dark had made me more afraid than I'd needed to be. We rumbled steadily along the country roads and I could turn my head and watch where we were going and see there wasn't really that much to be afraid of. My inside thigh muscles were giving me a sharp reminder of how tightly I'd been gripping with them the night before – they were absolutely killing me! I locked my fingers around Lucas's waist, feeling his soft skin under his thin T-shirt, and felt, well, kind of just a bit *amazing*.

We rode through a beautiful little town that went uphill in a spiral and I saw road-signs to Château-Gaillard, the place Lucas had mentioned, as we drove higher and higher, and then I saw it: a medieval castle. We stopped on a breezy plain where just a couple of cars were parked, and walked across to the castle ruins. The view was incredible, stretching for miles over hills and fields.

'This château was built by an Englishman,' Lucas said, getting all tour-guidey. 'Richard, *Coeur de Lion*.'

'The Lionheart,' I said, trying to sound clever. As we walked to the ruins, Lucas sank his hands into his pockets, pulling his jeans down a tiny bit, so I could see the top of his boxers, and carried on with the history lesson.

'It was created to be impregnable by the French. It stood here in our country, like a challenge to the natives. The proud English fortress. Untouched by the French assault.'

We crossed a series of stone bridges that were now sunk into grassy banks with steep slopes, where the land had begun to overgrow the ruins. Lucas pointed out strange wild flowers which he said had been brought here from the East during the crusades and still grew just here, within the castle's grounds, nowhere else in France. We came to an iron gate that closed off a dark, dungeon-like space, and Lucas stepped back and around in a kind of twirly way, positioning himself between me and the path out. He leaned forwards and I pressed back against the bars.

'But eventually, after much French persistence,' Lucas went on, 'we broke through the English defences. And took hold.' He was giving me the eyes again.

'I . . .'

'And conquered.'

I would have laughed out of embarrassment at the cheesiness if I hadn't been so *totally* thrilled. Lucas put a hand out and grabbed one of the bars behind me. He smiled.

'You look beautiful in this sunlight,' he said.

I'd been here before. Obviously not with Lucas. I

mean, between you and me, I have snogged quite a few boys. Just *snogged*, by the way. Two in one night, at the aforementioned party with the strong punch. Listen, I'm not recommending being a quite easy snog as a *good* thing – it's probably the opposite and has got me in plenty of trouble – but it has given me a bit of confidence in situations like this, and now I understood Lucas better than I had done before. I was still a bit trembly-kneed: the closeness of him, the scorch of his stare, it was all pretty powerful. I still wasn't *definitely* sure he was what I wanted, but knowing he liked me like that gave me back some sense of control.

There are a couple of ways of letting a boy know you're open to the idea of him kissing you, and I've found that the best is to look from their eyes to their lips. Eyes, lips, eyes, lips, and then touch your own lips very lightly, quite shyly, with your fingertips, as if you're kind of confused and nervous, but kissing is on your mind.

Yeah, it's a bit shameless. It works, though.

There's something quite magical about kissing outside in bright sunshine, because when you open your eyes, everything you see is sort of black and white, and it gradually comes back into colour like a Polaroid picture in front of you. And then you just want to close your eyes and start kissing all over again.

Afterwards, we walked back to his bike, holding hands.

'Last night in Vernon, I saw you waving at Bruno; do you know him?' Lucas asked softly. This is a terrible thing to own up to, but I really liked the jealousy that seemed to come with the question, it made me feel wanted.

'Do *you* know him?' I said, prolonging the moment.

'We went to school together,' he said, shrugging.

'Well, I had my bag stolen from a café in Vernon. And Bruno got it back for me. He just happened to be there. He's the only other person I've made friends with since I got here. Not like Rachel, who is, like, at the centre of the cool crowd. I don't seem to have her charm . . .'

'I would say you probably have more than you need,' Lucas said. Again with the cheese! But there is something about hearing cheesy lines in a French accent that makes you sort of melt. Heh, melted cheese. He smiled down at me. 'So, I have to go back to Paris. Do you want me to bring you?'

'Well, I think it's a bit late now,' I said. 'Maybe another day?'

'Why is it too late?' Lucas said.

'I'd have to get the train back, I'd hardly spend any time there.'

'You could stay over.' He talked casually, and quickly, as if everything he said was obvious and logical and everything I said didn't make much sense. But regardless, *that* was certainly not going to happen.

'No, I don't think your mum would go for that,' I said, laughing.

Lucas did a sort of . . . boy pout. Like a manly version of a girl pout – I think you can only do it with French lips. 'OK, well, I'll bring you into Vernon and you can do what you told my mother you were doing today. But I have to go to Paris.' Did he seem disappointed? Angry? Completely not bothered? He was back to being impossible to read. And damn, that was sexy.

Chapter 9

I found it nearly impossible to get to sleep that night, flipping crazily between regret and excitement. I'd snogged Lucas! My hosts' son! Thank *God* he went back to Paris rather than staying another night! Although, hey, by the way, how cool was I? Lucas was smoking hot!

Only, what was I going to do when he got back?

Eventually I did sleep, but when the morning came I'd barely woken up before I started worrying about what I'd done the day before. What was going to happen next? I'd tried calling Rachel as soon as Lucas had left for Paris, but she didn't answer her phone. She still didn't answer later that evening, when I sat on a lumpy little armchair in the corner of the Fayes' living room while they all watched telly, frantically checking my messages and hoping they didn't spot me doing it. By the next morning, Rachel still hadn't replied to any of my texts. I was feeling isolated again. As I came out of the bathroom, I came face to face with Chantal and felt myself turn absolutely beetroot red. There was no way she knew I'd been snogging her brother, but the blush was beyond my control. I gave her a stupid goofy smile and said, 'Hey,' but she just blinked at me drowsily.

I got dressed, went downstairs, and asked Madame Faye if she'd mind me skipping breakfast and leaving immediately. It was Sunday, and I knew they'd be going to church soon. Chantal, who was tearing up a croissant, asked if I wanted her bike again. I was starting to seriously love Chantal, she always came through. I texted Rachel again to tell her I was going into Vernon and she HAD to come out and meet me, and then I cycled over to my favourite café and waited.

I was looking down at my phone, waiting for Rachel's reply, and saw a shadow fall over my table. I thought it was the waiter with my cup of hot chocolate, so I was quite shocked to look up and see Bruno standing there instead. It was weird how I kept running into him . . . although admittedly one of the reasons I'd come back to this café – where I was *robbed*! – was that it was one of the first places in France I'd felt happy and not lonely, and that was because of him.

'Hi,' he said. 'May I join you?' I hesitated for a second too long, because he added. 'If you're waiting for someone, or you would just prefer to be alone . . .' As usual, I found it really sweet the way he talked in that old-fashioned way, like someone in a black and white film.

'Oh no, I'd be deligh—' I stopped myself replying the same way. 'I mean, yeah, that'd be great.'

I was glad he was there – sitting alone in a café only felt romantic and independent the first couple of times you did it, before you started getting jealous of all the people with, you know, friends. But although he was really nice to talk to, I thought Bruno maybe fancied me a little bit, which changed things. Now I'd snogged someone else, it felt weirder talking to him. On the one hand, the pressure was off. If things were edging towards the romantic, I could tell him I was interested in someone else. On the other hand, part of me definitely didn't want to mention Lucas, as it'd ruin the gentle, flirty way we'd talked when we last had breakfast here together. Spending time with Bruno made me feel good, like the cup of hot chocolate that the waiter finally gave me. In comparison, spending time with Lucas was more like strong coffee – a lot less sweet and left me twitchy, but somehow felt more grown up and sophisticated.

'So do you have breakfast here every day?' I asked him.

'Not every day,' he said. 'But it's a nice place to sit outside and sketch.' I noticed he had a sketchbook with him, and he flashed it open to a random page to show me. It was full of faces – people who might have sat in the café near him. They were simple and really good, a few lines perfectly conveying the tiredness of an old man, or a lady eating a croissant at the exact moment her stiff snobbiness melted into greed. But he closed it just as quickly, telling me, 'They're not very good.'

'I wouldn't say that,' I said.

Bruno changed the subject, asking me what I'd been up to and seen since I arrived, and I gave him a long list of Faye activities.

'Oh, you're staying with the Fayes?' he said, and I realised too late that I'd casually insulted them for being strict and boring, when I should have thought that he went to school with Lucas and they could all be family friends.

'They are really nice, actually,' I blustered. 'It's just that I'm not so interested in all the traditional touristy things they've been showing me. It's my fault, though, for being a bit of a lightweight. I mean . . .' I couldn't think of an alternative to lightweight, and couldn't imagine a Frenchman knowing what it meant. 'I mean, I'm not all that intelligent.'

'I wouldn't say that,' Bruno said, with a grin. 'You get along with Chantal, though?'

'Oh yeah, she's great. But I'm not sure Chantal has as much time for me. I think I've been foisted on her. She's had to babysit for me when she'd rather be off practising with her band for this summer festival thing she's doing.'

'The Fouenne festival. Yes, I . . .' Bruno smiled, looking embarrassed. 'I have some friends who are involved with that. Well, *I* am involved with that.'

'No, really? What are you doing?'

'Not very much. I promised my sister. I have a small part in a play she and her friends wrote for it.'

'Cool, I'll get to see it,' I said.

Bruno covered his face with his hands. 'I think I'd prefer that you didn't. There will be . . .' he trailed off as if trying to find the word in English.

I tilted my head on one side. 'Nudity?' I said, naughtily.

'Worse. Medieval costumes,' Bruno said, wincing. 'And . . . *dancing*.'

I giggled. '*You'll* be dancing? OK, there's *no way* I'm not going to come and see this now. Anyway, I have to support Chantal, I've been watching her rehearsals. How old is your sister?'

'Claudine? She's sixteen.'

We started talking about his little sister and how he thought she was a lot cooler than him. Then sort of out of the blue, Bruno said, 'And Lucas, how do you get on with him?'

For the second time that day I felt my cheeks redden instantly. Same reason. I started to gabble something about only having seen a little of him because he'd spent most of the time in Paris, but Bruno stopped me.

72

'It's OK, I'm not . . . I don't mean to be intrusive.' He'd obviously guessed at something near the truth. I looked down into my empty cup.

'Really, I don't know him very well,' I said. 'I don't know what's going on.'

'It's not my business,' Bruno said, quietly. For the first time, our conversation dried up and I looked around the café for something to talk about. 'But he's . . .' Bruno began again. 'I think, I think you should make sure you know about him if you want to see more of him.'

'What do you mean?'

Bruno suddenly looked angry, but with himself. 'I don't mean anything bad. Forgive me. He's, well you know, he's older than you, that's all. I'm being stupid. Please forget I said anything.'

My phone pipped with a message from Rachel.

'Do you want to answer your phone?' Bruno said. 'I've remembered I promised to buy Claudine something while I was out – perhaps you could watch my bag for a moment till I get back? I mean . . .' – and the smile came back to his face – 'better than you watch your own bag?'

I smiled too. 'Yep, no problem.'

He left the café, leaving his rucksack and sketching stuff on the table. Rachel's text said, *Whatsup?* I texted, *OK to call?* She texted, *Yes*.

'I have got to see you!' I said, when she answered my call. 'I'm in Vernon now – what are you doing today?'

'I've got to see you too!' Rachel said. 'I can come out – where are you?'

'I'm at the Café Georges.'

'Right, it'll take me about fifteen minutes to get out and down to you,' she said.

'OK, come on, then! Hurry,' I said, laughing, just mainly out of delight that I was finally going to see my friend again. I drummed my fingers with excitement, and then carelessly opened Bruno's sketch book, without even thinking about whether it was a bad thing to do. On one of the early pages was an utterly gorgeous line drawing of – well, it was . . . *me*. I mean, it was gorgeously done, the subject wasn't gorgeous! Well . . . you know, I did look kind of pretty . . . But it was so sweet. He must have done it the day he rescued my bag, before he met me, when I was just another stranger in a café. I snapped the book shut immediately and fought the urge to take a longer look.

When Bruno came back, I blushed *yet again*, and told him my friend was on her way, and he was welcome to stay and meet her, but he rather sensitively said he had to make a move, and that he hoped he saw me again before I left. We swapped numbers. When he was gone, I felt unexpectedly sad, almost close to tears, but I couldn't really make much sense of that at all.

Chapter 10

Rachel turned up more than *three-quarters* of a bloody hour later, and because I was waiting for her I felt much more self-conscious than I would have being alone on purpose. I'd already spent quite a while in the café with Bruno, and I worried the waiters were sick of the sight of me. Towards the end of the wait, I worried Rachel wasn't going to come at all, and my weird tearful-out-of-nowhere feeling just seemed to get worse; so by the time she *did* arrive I wanted to sulk. But I was just too happy to see her.

'Yayyy!' I said, immediately feeling a bit stupid.

'OK, so what's the news, and then I have to tell you mine!' she said before she'd even sat down.

I didn't *want* to rush. I wanted to feel normal with her again first and get back to where we'd been. Somehow, she was almost like a stranger, or anyway a different version of herself. She seemed louder and everything about her was fast and impatient.

'No, you first' I said. 'It sounds serious.' Even though it had been me repeatedly texting and calling her and getting no reply. But I could sense how much she wanted to talk about something.

'Uuuuuuh, I . . . talk to me first.'

'OK, well, yesterday, Lucas took me to a château on his moped – I ride his bike now, like that's normal, ha ha! – and we ended up snogging for quite a while.' I paused and looked straight at her.

'I had sex with Fabrice,' Rachel said.

'WHAT? You HAVE had?'

'Yes.'

'When?'

'Two days ago. The night we were all here in town. The night you met him.'

'But you don't even *know* him!'

'Wow, you're really making me feel great,' Rachel said. Her eyes looked teary. My stomach lurched with guilt; I felt horrible.

'I'm sorry, Rach. I'm just shocked. How do you feel?'

'Fine. I'm not sure.'

'Well, it was what you wanted, wasn't it?'

'Yeah, of course.'

I moved my chair round to her side of the table and we leaned against each other, shoulder to shoulder, not talking for a bit.

'So what happened?' I said at last.

'I went home with him, his parents were away, we drank some calvados – that's this insanely strong apple liqueur they make here, apparently – and we ended up, you know.'

'How drunk were you?'

'I shouldn't have got drunk,' Rachel said. 'But I knew what I was doing.'

'What about Madame Lacasse? Didn't she ask why you didn't come back?'

'I told her I was staying with you,' Rachel said.

'Oh. Oh wow,' I said.

'Well, you're not going to deny it!' she said.

'No, of course not,' I said. 'I was just thinking, you know, what if your Frenchwoman gets together and talks to my Frenchwoman. Well, I guess there's no reason they would, I'm being crazy. Oh listen, you have to come round to dinner at ours soon, Madame Faye told me to ask you.'

'Yeah, of course I will,' Rachel said absently.

'So . . . do you want to talk about it?'

'Well, you know how it works,' Rachel said.

'Well, you know I don't!' I said. I leaned back in my chair, moving it away from her. I felt exhausted. I was cross with her for not talking about this to me sooner, although I wasn't sure when she could have. BEFORE, maybe? She was my best friend! At the same time I was scared of her and scared *for* her. I thought she'd done a really stupid thing. She didn't know Fabrice well enough. They lived in different countries. 'And how do you feel about *him*?' I said.

She picked up the annoyance in my voice and turned back to me looking angrier. 'What if I'm in love with him?' she asked me loudly. 'Is that good enough for you? Or do you have a problem with how easily I did it?'

'I didn't say anything like that!'

'You're thinking it.'

'I am NOT THINKING IT!'

'Oh.'

'I'm just worried about you.'

'You know, Sam,' Rachel said, and I could sense her sort of toughening up against me, 'it's not that big a deal. It's just the next step. And this holiday was supposed to be about having fun and falling in love and getting out and living. And when I look back on my life, I will be able to say that I lost my virginity one summer in France to an absolutely gorgeous French boy who I was totally crazy about, and it was romantic and exciting and . . .'

'And that's *fantastic*!' I said. 'I just didn't want you to —'

' . . . and terrifying and painful and maybe a mistake,' she finished, more quietly.

I felt guilty again. 'It's not a mistake,' I said, trying

78

to remember that I should be supportive before anything else. 'Like you say, it's not that big a deal. Half the girls we know have.'

'Maybe not half.'

'Maybe half!'

'Maybe not girls like me.' Rachel sighed. I didn't know what to say, I didn't know what she wanted to hear from me. She was right, girls like her didn't do this. She'd had one boyfriend the whole time I'd known her, and yet, she was the one who'd lost her virginity, in a flash. To a holiday romance.

'Well,' I began carefully, and then couldn't think of anything comforting. 'Was it really painful?'

'Yeah.'

'And how did you leave things? I mean, do you want to keep seeing him?'

'Yeah, *of course!*'

'So, what's going to happen?'

'Oh, just leave it, Sam! This is not the conversation I want to be having!'

I was confused and angry. 'I don't know what conversation you want to be having. Maybe you should just have it and I'll sit and listen and nod.'

We sat in silence for ages.

'So you snogged Lucas?' Rachel said, half-smiling, as if this was a peace offering. 'And . . . what's going to happen?'

I laughed. 'Well, you kind of stole my thunder.'

'He's lovely,' Rachel said.

'I don't know about that,' I said. I started talking about Lucas because it seemed easier after that edgy stand-off to talk about myself, but when I went into more detail about the romantic things that had happened when we went to the castle, Rachel kept interrupting with stories of how romantic Fabrice had been. Sometimes, weirdly, it felt like a competition. It had never felt like that between us before.

'Listen, when are you going to come round to dinner with the Fayes?' I said. 'Madame Faye seemed very keen. As I said, it makes sense to have *met* her if you're going to use her as an excuse.'

'Yeah. But you've made it sound so *terrible*,' Rachel said. 'I can't eat five courses of minging food.' I noticed for the first time that Rachel had lost some weight.

'Are you dieting?' I asked.

'I'm always dieting,' Rachel said. 'Do you mean, is it working?'

'You just seem *different*,' I said. 'I haven't seen you for a few days and now . . . everything's different.'

'Sometimes different is good,' Rachel said.

The conversation got a bit awkward and when Rachel went to the loo, I sat and got more stressed. She was overtaking me, and I was worried I was handling it badly. What I'd said about half the girls we knew was true – and maybe I was running out of time before I'd start to look like some kind of freak among our friends. I knew I wasn't ready to take that step, but I also didn't want to be the last one who did. Rachel had always been my safety net. She was my nice friend who didn't get involved in that sort of thing. She was careful, she'd never even wasted her time snogging some boy she didn't really go for, the way I sometimes had, just so I could say I'd pulled someone at every party, like some kind of badge of pride.

But unlike Rachel, I'd had steady boyfriends too, and the issue had obviously come up a lot more for me. But what was I holding back for? Why *was* this a problem for me? I'd always made it clear to boys I went out with that it wasn't on the cards, and hadn't even allowed any discussion on the subject. Really, I knew the answer: I'd never been in love. I liked going out with boys, but I hadn't fallen hard for any of them, and there was no way I was going to have sex with someone I didn't love. I'd always believed Rachel felt the same and, maybe stupidly, always assumed I would be the first out of the two of us to make that move. It was possible that Rachel *did* love Fabrice, but it still seemed too quick. I thought briefly about the slightly spooky advice Bruno had given to me earlier that morning, to make sure I 'knew' about Lucas. The thing about the boys back home was that we really did know them, we'd been going to school with them all our lives. How could she trust Fabrice?

When Rachel came back, she said she had to go home to get ready, because she was meeting Fabrice later. I cycled home, my head messed up with the shock of all the news. When my phone rang, I guessed it was Rachel, wanting to smooth over our weird chat, but it was Lucas – I'd given him my number. He asked if I wanted to catch a train to Paris the next day to hang out with him. Two days before, I'd have leaped at the chance. Now, everything about these French boys seemed to be moving too quickly for me, and it felt like there were no brakes – you had the choice of staying on or jumping off, nothing else. I was regretting kissing Lucas. I didn't know if I'd even really liked him, or if I was just enjoying that buzz you get when you make a boy start liking you.

'Yesterday at the château was really great,' I began. 'But I feel like maybe we jumped into things a bit too soon . . .'

Lucas laughed, and I felt mortified. 'I'm not proposing marriage,' he said. 'I thought we were friends, and it would be fun. Another time, little girl.'

I was *furious* . . . 'little girl'! But also I was dying of embarrassment. What had I been *thinking*, trying to give him a serious break up speech like that? All we'd done was kiss. I'd lost all sense of perspective and was acting like a lunatic. I needed to get a grip. Not everyone is having sex, Sam, I told myself, and then I went and hid under my bedclothes. I'd had enough of everything for one day.

Chapter 11

Rachel came round to the Faye house for dinner the next day, to my delight and amazement. The really big shock was that she could talk French now! My French hadn't improved very much at all. Madame Faye made me talk French to her, but all the French people *my* age had much better English, and I'd lazily let them speak it all the time. Rachel was rattling off her answers to Madame Faye's questions as if she'd been here a year. We went up to my room to talk while dinner was being prepared, and I asked her how she'd got so good.

'I dunno,' she said. 'You just get used to using some phrases a lot, don't you?'

Um, *no*.

'So, you've seen more of Fabrice?' I said. Rachel smiled. 'Listen,' I said, really quickly, 'I think I came over as weird on Sunday and I really wasn't . . . I didn't mean to make you think I disapproved or thought it was a bad idea, I was just shocked, and shocked for myself as much as for you, not that it was shocking, it's just, you know, now it feels like everyone is moving on to the next stage, if you are – I don't mean that you would have less reason to than anyone else, but you know, you're *Rachel*, you don't do that kind of thing, like you said–'

'Sam,' Rachel said, laughing, 'take a breath!'

'I was just *worried* about us,' I said. 'We never fall out!'

'When did we fall out?' she said, frowning as if she was trying really hard to remember.

'Well, when you told me about . . . Fabrice, and I was shocked, and you said I was acting as if you'd rushed things, when that wasn't what I meant to say at all.'

'I understood how you were feeling,' Rachel said, in a cool, smooth way. 'It was completely fine, I knew it was a lot to lay on you in one go. I should have given you more of a status report on the way, but you know how things have been since we got here, it's been nearly impossible to keep in touch the way we thought we would. I've been rushing around with Victoire and her friends and you've been shut up here with the Addams Family.'

I was relieved that she was being nice, but it was totally frustrating that she was denying there'd been any problem with our conversation. I wanted to sort things out and make sure we were OK again. And I'd believed I'd really hurt her feelings when we talked about Fabrice. But now she was just acting puzzled and amused as if it had all been in my head – while reminding me of how terrific her life was.

'What's that smell?' Rachel said.

The unmistakable odour of boingy grey fish had made it upstairs.

'Dinner,' I said.

'It smells like old fish bones being melted into glue.'

'Yeah, it tastes like that too.'

'You are kidding.'

'Why would it taste any different?'

Rachel gagged. 'Seriously, you are kidding. It's not going to taste like that. That fish must be six weeks old.'

'Just eat what you can,' I said, suddenly finding it funny.

'I'm going to pop down and tell her I'm a vegetarian.'

'You're going to what?'

'She'll just make me a salad. I can't eat that fish. Just the smell is making me sick. Anyway, she likes me, my French is good.'

So Rachel vanished downstairs and I sneaked to the landing so I could listen. I could hear her apologising with her amazing new French, and letting Madame Faye know that she didn't eat meat or fish, and hoped she hadn't put her hostess out, as she'd meant to give her notice and could eat *anything* else. Madame Faye asked her some questions, sounding confused, then definitely irritated. Rachel answered, laughing. I thought that might be a dangerous idea. But she joined me back upstairs looking pleased with herself.

'It's fine,' she said, 'I don't have to eat the fish! Poor you, though.'

'Seriously, promise me you're not on some crazy diet,' I said. 'You should know you look fantastic the way you are.'

'I promise I'm not,' she said. 'You *can* smell that fish, can't you? Your senses haven't died from spending two weeks in this house?'

I laughed, finally. 'OK, not wanting to eat Faye fish is not the sign of an eating disorder. Listen, I should stop worrying about you, you have everything under control, you have a gorgeous boyfriend, you look great, and you can speak French.'

'Yay,' Rachel said. 'I *am* really happy. This holiday is the most amazing thing we ever did. I'm really glad you made us come here.'

The truth? I was so jealous of her it hurt.

Argh, what was wrong with me? I didn't want to sleep with French boys I hardly knew! I just wanted to feel like *I* knew what I was doing, like Rachel. I wanted to believe I knew what I wanted, too. I . . . just wanted *her* holiday, for it all to be as exciting and life-changing for me, for something to happen to *me too*.

Chantal had been helping with dinner and she came in to tell us it was ready. Rachel talked to her in scary-fast French, and I felt like an idiot for making her talk English to me. But I could sense Chantal wasn't warming to Rachel all that much. She had that half-smile, the one she'd originally greeted me with, where you couldn't tell whether she was just wary of you or laughing at you.

Monsieur Faye poured us all wine. The French just regularly give their teenage children wine, which is pretty cool. Having said that, it was really sour, almost like vinegar, and I couldn't drink it. The jelly-covered paté came out and Rachel daintily (and with a rather smug glance at me) thanked Madame Faye and turned it down, filling up on dry bread and butter. Then the fish, and I looked at Rachel and she gave me a tiny wink. After putting it down in the middle of the table, Madame Faye went back to the kitchen and came back with an enormous plate for Rachel: a huge pile of sliced pickled gherkins, giant, hairy pickled onions, and chopped up hard boiled eggs, with dark grey yolks. There were about five eggs altogether. Gosh, I hoped she wasn't meeting Fabrice tonight. I noticed Chantal looked even more amused; I think she had some idea of Rachel's horror.

After dinner, Rachel said she was going to call Madame Lacasse for a lift home but Monsieur Faye insisted he'd take her. This was rapidly turning into a nightmare evening for Rachel. If I sat in the car with her, it would have meant another trip home alone with Monsieur Faye for me, but I owed it to her as my best friend. But . . . in the end the decision was made for me. Madame Faye told me she wanted to have a word with me, and that I didn't need to accompany my friend; she would be perfectly all right.

When Rachel left, Madame Faye *had* that word. She delivered a seemingly endless lecture in angry French: I had been lazy and untidy since I got there, I never helped her with any of the meals or any of the clearing up, or any housework. I was rude and disappeared to do my own thing when she was supposed to be looking after me and 'educating' me. I preferred to go out on Lucas's moped. More than anything, I was ungrateful. If my attitude didn't change, she planned to call my mother to tell her the situation was not working out and I had better go home a week or two early. Right at that moment, there was nothing I wanted more. I had to fight hard not to cry; it had been a long time since I'd been told off like this by anyone. In a way, she was right, I had been keeping myself to myself. And after dinner, I always made myself scarce, because I didn't like being in the way, and when I stuck around trying to be helpful the Fayes would start barking at each other in really angry French – I mean, they were talking about work, and other people they knew; they weren't angry at me, but it was difficult being around them, and they didn't really speak to me. And, seeing as I'd only just worked out how to work the *toilet*, there was no way I was going to tackle the washing machine, and I did try to keep all my stuff tidy. It had been really difficult to work out what was expected of me. I didn't say any of this, though – I just looked up at her and nodded.

Madame Faye finally left me alone, and I did cry. Chantal came in and I tried to hide it. But Chantal was very cool about the crying, acting as if she hadn't even noticed. She just said, 'Let's clean this kitchen, eh?' and turned on the radio to some station with her usual weird indie music on it, and we didn't talk, we just worked together. I was *so* grateful to her, for not making a big deal about it, for helping me, and most of all, just for being there with me.

When we were hanging up the tea-towels, though, straight out of the blue, she asked me if I was letting Lucas seduce me. That was how she put it: letting him seduce me. I said I hadn't seen that much of him, but there'd been some flirting. She understood the word perfectly, maybe she even understood it the way I meant it. She looked at me with her eyebrow raised, not smiling, not annoyed, just trying to get me.

'I don't think it will happen again,' I told her. I said it because it was what I thought she wanted to hear. But as I was saying it, I realised it was what *I* wanted to hear, and even though it was me saying it, hearing it felt like being reassured by a friend.

Chapter 12

'OK, no ifs, no buts, no excuses, you're coming to Paris with me today.'

Rachel had called at ten to seven, waking me up. I quickly swapped my early morning confusion for excitement.

'Just you and me? How are we going to get there? The train?'

'Yeah yeah. How quickly can you get into Vernon? Is there anyone who'll give you a lift?'

I thought about the evening before – Madame Faye telling me I was lazy and ungrateful and that she was considering sending me home if I didn't start changing my attitude. This wasn't going to be easy to arrange. My heart fell.

'Listen, I can't do it. I could get into town in about an hour, but old lady Faye was right on my back last night. She gave me grief for ages about how badly I'm behaving. I mean, what time would we get back?'

'No, we're going to stay in Paris overnight. There's a *party*!'

'*Whose* party?'

'It's some friends of friends – you know Marthe? It's her big sister. She's a student. They have a flat there, so we can stay the night – they've got plenty of room.' How had my shy friend made friends in *Paris* after spending two weeks in the French *countryside*?

'I think I'd better not,' I said. 'Not only will old Mother Faye go nuts, but if it's going to be you, me and Fabrice, I think I'd better say no. I'm going to feel like a total idiot.'

There was a silence.

'I don't know if Fabrice is going,' Rachel said. 'He still might, but I think it's not that likely.'

'Why?'

'He's just busy,' Rachel said. 'Anyway, I'm not going to leave you alone, and it's time we had some fun together. Pack a bag and tell Mother Faye.'

Unsurprisingly, the Paris plan didn't go down too well with Madame Faye after the warning she'd given me the evening before, but I just kept repeating that I would be safe, that I'd be back the next morning, that we wanted to see as much of France as possible while we were here, including all the famous art galleries and museums, and that I wanted to buy my mum a fancy present from Paris. Anyway, I was seventeen, what right did she have to stop me? OK, I didn't actually say that, I didn't want to push it.

I met Rachel at Vernon station, and we went on to Paris. It was about two weeks since we'd ridden this train in the other direction, but that weird time-runs-slowly holiday effect made me feel really tired. If I could have stayed on the train while it took me all the way back home to England, I would have.

Rachel's notebook was full of suggestions for places to go, made by all her French friends, and she tried to work out a schedule for us, but I didn't really have anything to say or any opinion to offer; I could only sit there, nodding, saying 'Yeah, that sounds great' to everything she mentioned.

We hadn't seen anything of Paris on the way to Normandy, we'd just run around changing trains and grabbing sandwiches and drinks and wacky French chocolate bars. I'd never been to Paris before. I fell in love with it straight away. *So beautiful!* The French must come to England and see all the square, plain buildings and wonder how a country can look so boring. I was so happy to be there that it was almost breaking my heart that we wouldn't have enough time to do and see everything, not even *anything*, really. There were the touristy places, like the Eiffel Tower, and the river and the parks, and now I was here I wanted to do all of those, but they weren't on Rachel's list. The list had been drawn up for her by a bunch of cool French girls, and as Rachel said, it would be a waste of our time queueing up with a bunch of stupid middle-aged Americans just so we could physically stand in places we'd seen in films a million times. I had to admit it was better to stick to the list, and to go straight in as a Parisian.

'We can come back,' Rachel reminded me, 'We're still here for another two weeks.'

She was right, of course, and I admitted it while we were sipping *citrons pressés* and eating little pink cakes that looked like works of art in a tiny café with gold-edged chairs and painted walls. I was still admitting it – but now silently to myself – as we walked straight past all the usual chains – the Zaras and H&Ms – and slipped in and out of tiny boutiques with crazy-trendy shoes and dresses like nothing I'd seen before. It was so exciting that a weird fizzy, happy feeling welled up inside me, and I thought I wouldn't be able to keep it inside and I'd have to laugh out loud like a crazy person just to ease the pressure. But as the day wore on, that feeling started to fade. We started trying things on, and Rachel seemed sort of *extra* loud, asking the assistants questions in French, making jokes with them and telling me things 'really wouldn't work with your colouring'. It felt a lot like showing off. She *was* being funny, and I was, once again, knocked out by how cool she was. I couldn't help remembering the time I took her shopping for her first proper date with Ginger Brian, talking her out of buying a hideous pair of 'urban' shorts (while smothering my giggles at what she looked like in them) before steering her towards a cute top and jeans. Now look at us. I was mad at myself, not her, for not being able to be happy for her. Next to her, I felt myself fading.

'So, look, where are we staying? Shouldn't we check in with them, tell them we're here, and maybe we could drop our bags off there?' I asked her. We were resting our tired feet while drowning in sunshine in the Palais Royal gardens, a quiet rectangular park with fountains and leafy trees, surrounded by shops that sold things like puppets and vintage dresses.

'Yes, she said to call after five,' Rachel said. 'Don't worry. Although . . .'

She flipped open her phone, called a number and got no answer, then tapped out and sent a text.

'Is that to Fabrice?' I asked. Rachel nodded.

I watched two tiny French schoolgirls walking solemnly round a fountain, holding hands. I thought of me and Rachel before our lives started being about exams and boys and having to get everything right and make choices.

The phone rang. Rachel answered, '*Allo, oueh?*' '*Oueh*' rhymes with 'yeah' – it was the way the French girls we knew said *oui*. Blimey, she even answered the phone in French. She didn't say much, just 'oueh' a lot, and when she hung up she turned her head in the other direction and said, 'Well, that's good news, Fabrice isn't coming, so it'll just be you and me hanging out. It'll be fun.' But she didn't sound happy.

'How *are* things with him?' I said.

'I don't know,' Rachel said. 'Maybe I should have . . . I don't know. I mean, it turns out he might have a girlfriend for one thing.'

'WHAT?'

'Yeah, but I don't know for sure how serious it is.'

'But when did you find out?'

'Well, I sort of knew. It's not really a *problem*.'

'How is it not a problem? I thought you thought you loved him.'

Rachel blew the hair out of her eyes. 'It's been an intense couple of weeks,' she said.

'OK, who are you and what have you done with Rachel?' I said, trying to make a joke of it.

'Oh, don't say that!' she said. 'You make me feel like I've really disappointed you.'

'Of course I'm not disappointed. If anything . . . I'm really jealous of you,' I said – and it was true for a lot of things, although I didn't envy the situation she was in with Fabrice, and I didn't really understand how she'd found herself there.

'Why would you be jealous? Because I lost my virginity and you didn't? And you could have at any time, so what difference does it make? All this obsessing over it, and I promise you, when it happens, it's . . . it's such a big deal but it's also *nothing*. What I mean is, I wish I had let it be a big deal, and I didn't, and now it never will be, and it could have been. Do you know what I mean?'

I did know, but I didn't want her to feel worse. 'You've come out of yourself so much since we got here,' I said. 'You're confident, you look fantastic, you're turning heads, everyone is, like, *dazzled* by you. This is the holiday we came here to have. I don't know what's going to happen with Fabrice, but you can't regret it. How have you left things?'

'Part of me just doesn't want to see him again. The rest of me wishes he really loved me.'

'Well . . .' I had no idea what I should be telling her. 'You sound like you don't know what you want.'

'I *don't* know! As soon as he started acting more distant, I realised I barely even knew him, and . . . I can't really explain. I've opened myself up to someone I don't know if I can trust and I just want to forget the whole thing and hide. But I still fancy the boy I fell for and want him to come back and be the person I thought he was.'

'We don't have to go to this party tonight,' I said. 'Shall we just go home?'

'No, let's have fun,' Rachel said. 'Let's just forget everything and have an excellent night.'

She leaned back in the park's little metal chair, facing the sun, and closed her eyes, and I watched her face without her knowing, until the frown line in the middle of her forehead disappeared.

Chapter 13

Marthe's sister lived in Montmartre, high on a hill at the top of Paris, and we got there by going up about a million stairs towards the Sacré Coeur, a huge white church that looked like the Taj Mahal. At the top we were both completely puffed out, and sat on the church steps looking out over the whole city. I could see the Eiffel Tower, and Notre Dame, and all the touristy places we'd been too hip to go to. It was the early evening, and there seemed to be loads of people our age sitting around in groups. A boy with a guitar serenaded some pretty girls, backpackers unrolled sleeping-mats and took out sandwiches. I told Rachel about the idiot way I'd acted with Lucas – first kissing him at the castle, then suddenly panicking and trying to formally put him off. And the way he'd laughed at me and called me 'little girl'. Sharing a bit of embarrassment seemed to cheer Rachel up, although she said he was the one who'd acted like an idiot, not me. I think she was glad to have the pressure taken off her love life, and also we'd slipped back a bit to being how we used to be together – I'd been the one with boy troubles, she'd listened and advised.

'He's somewhere here in the city tonight, I guess,' I said, then a scary thought struck me. 'You don't think he'll be at the party, do you? He knows Marthe.'

'Dunno, maybe,' Rachel said. 'You'd be OK seeing him, though, wouldn't you? You, queen of snogging, can face people after snogging them. Or, let's face it, you wouldn't be able to talk to half the boys in the Sixth Form.'

'True,' I said. How weird it was that I'd been so confident back home just a few weeks before, and now here I was an absolute beginner again. 'Anyway, he's going to be home again before I go, so I'll have to face him some time. It may as well be tonight.'

'Well, Marthe didn't mention him being there. They all know each other, though, everyone who went to that school.'

'I hope we all stay in touch after we leave school,' I said.

'*We* will,' Rachel said. The boy with the guitar was singing a Beatles song in French. The problems that had been nagging at me all holiday seemed muffled here, as if I'd sealed them in bubble wrap and put them to one side. I was aware of how big the future was and felt suddenly warm and cold all over. It was one of those amazing moments when you want to hold your breath because just maybe it will stop time, and you can stay there.

Marthe answered the door at her sister's flat, and she and Rachel kissed on both cheeks, while I stood a step or two behind, wondering if I'd do the same when I didn't really know her at all. She did kiss me, but I mis-timed, and banged my cheek against hers a bit hard. She spoke in quick French to Rachel, but I could basically understand almost all of it – she was saying it was such a shame Madame Lacasse hadn't let Victoire come over, and that the boy she, Marthe, fancied, was already here and Rachel had to come and take a look. It felt strange, my friend having friends I hardly knew – this whole extra life all of a sudden.

It was a big, old-fashioned and very messy flat, spread over two floors above a restaurant. We dropped our bags in a dark bedroom on the top floor, then came down again. There were eight or nine people in the room other than us, girls and boys, and the unmistakable smell of pot, although the smokers just seemed to be smoking normal cigarettes. Apart from Marthe, they were all a few years older than us. I sat on a futon with Rachel and sipped wine – but I had no intention of getting drunk. I felt like a little kid. I couldn't talk in French to these people, I didn't have anything to contribute, already it felt like a *big* mistake, but it was too late to go home. I hoped Rachel somehow felt like I did, and that the two of us could maybe just go back upstairs, spend the night chatting together as we sipped our wine, get some sleep, and then set off in the morning. That didn't happen.

When the room got dark, a lot more people arrived, and someone turned the stereo up about fifty times louder. The floor filled up with people sitting with their legs out and draped all over each other, shouting to be heard above the music. There was a thick, fuggy smoke, and I felt sick. Rachel had started talking to the boy on her left – in English for a change – and I pretended to be listening and interested, just to look less stupid, less like a spare part. I was both incredibly bored and uncomfortably self-conscious at the same time. Mainly I was just thinking: I want to leave; I want to go; I have to get out of here. Even more unexpectedly, I wished I'd stayed with Chantal, and that I was back home with the Fayes.

Hours passed. No exaggeration: *hours*. Rachel had carried on drinking; I hadn't touched any more of my wine. I needed some water, but I was scared to move, because I thought I'd draw attention to myself. Then the boy Rachel was talking to, who kept looking straight at me in a way I interpreted as meaning, 'Who the hell are you and why don't you go away now?' just started stroking Rachel's leg. She didn't stop him. He leaned in to whisper to her. It was pretty obvious they were about to start making out. I'd been in a similar situation in parties at home with Rachel, and I had just snogged the bloke. Now, in what had once been Rachel's position, I realised how *seriously* selfish this was. I understood what it was like to be the friend who isn't snogging. Except, when I'd done this in the past, it had been at friends' houses, and we both knew the boy. That meant Rachel didn't need to worry about leaving me, the way I was worried about abandoning her now, just as much as I was worried about staying and being in the way.

They started kissing, of course, and I looked around the room for Marthe and couldn't find her. Lucas hadn't come, despite my worries that he would – and right then I'd have given anything to see another face I knew. I definitely couldn't pretend I was taking part in Rachel's conversation now, so I went to the kitchen to get the water I'd been craving. Marthe and her older sister were there, thank *God*, and I told them I was feeling kind of sick and would they mind if I just went to bed right now?

Marthe's sister stubbed out her cigarette on a saucer and took me upstairs. There was a squashed-looking bed with dirty, rumpled sheets in the room where we'd left our bags, and she cheerfully pointed it out.

'The bathroom's just across there. Can I get you some aspirins?' she asked me gently. I think she thought I was really young, and felt sorry for me.

'Oh, yes please, thanks,' I said, because I wanted her to come back and talk to me a little longer. She brought them in and sat down on the bed with me. It dipped in the middle, scarily, with both our weights on it.

'Don't worry, I'll keep an eye on your friend for you,' she said. She was *so sweet*. I got into bed and despite the deafening, pulsing music from downstairs, I found myself falling asleep.

'*QU'ARRIVE-T-IL ? QUI ÊTES VOUS?*'

The shouting was right in my face, and I woke with absolute terror, my heart bursting out of my throat. I had no idea where I was, I couldn't see, and I thought I was going to die from fear. There was some boy I didn't know shouting at me in French. I couldn't even remember I was in France, I had never been so scared in my life.

'*C'EST MON LIT!*' he kept shouting. He was drunk and angry. I was rescued – *again* – by Marthe's older sister, who was babysitting me for the night, and she came in and grabbed the drunk boy by the shoulders and explained who I was and why she'd put me in his bed. Then she got angry with him, telling him he'd said he wasn't going to be back tonight, and he started apologising, then apologising to me, shouting just as loudly, telling me I could sleep there if I wanted. At this point I thought I would never sleep again as long as I lived. He staggered round the room drunkenly, telling me in English, 'Perhaps I squeeze in later with you?' and smiling. He was no longer as frightening, but he was big and clumsy. Marthe's sister dragged him out. But I couldn't stay there now. I pulled my jeans on over my pyjamas, and thought about going to find Rachel, but I was in too much of a state, she'd have thought I'd gone crazy, and I didn't want to interrupt her snog like this, looking like a six-year-old who'd just had a nightmare. I found another empty room, sat down on the floor between the bed and the wardrobe, and cried out all the bad, until my heart slowed down, but I didn't really stop shaking.

Chapter 14

Don't ruin Paris, I kept telling myself. Yesterday was lovely – well, all *day* was – optimistic for the future but also like old times – before things went bad-party-bad. If you *have* to fight with her now, you lose the day too. I stared out of the train window at the weird French electricity pylons in the fields, which looked like alien robot invaders. Don't ruin Paris.

'Are you sure you're OK?' Rachel said again.

'Yeah,' I said, in an annoyingly weedy voice. 'I'm just really tired.' But I could hear myself sounding angry and judgemental and knew she felt bad and my weediness would make her feel worse. I kept thinking of ways I could tell her off and managed to stop myself saying them. In the end, nothing that *bad* had happened. Besides, how many terrible parties back home had I forced her to stay to the end of just because I'd had a crush on some loser there? But we were in France, and everything was different, and – once again – *Rachel* wasn't supposed to do that sort of thing. I'd ended up not sleeping on Marthe's sister's floor, next to Marthe, on a couple of thickly folded blankets that didn't soften the hard wooden floorboards very much, and Rachel had stayed up the whole night 'talking' to the French boy. That was her official account of things – she said she might have dozed off with him on the sofa, she couldn't really remember. I was tired, maybe that was really why I was angry. I felt empty and sick, and my head was filled with unyawned yawns that pulled at my cheeks.

The train was practically silent. Rachel tried a few times to start a conversation, but the heavy quiet around us sort of crushed her into embarrassment and she ended up whispering. I started to feel sorry for her, and wanted to let her know I really was fine, but I couldn't think of anything to say. So, I just smiled when we split up at Vernon, and told her to keep in touch and text me. I practically sleepwalked back to the Fayes' house, letting my feet remember the way because my head had checked out.

If I'd known what was going to greet me, I think I'd have gone straight back in the other direction. Madame Faye was furious, *again*. So angry, she was talking in English, to make sure I didn't miss a word. It seemed Madame Lacasse had called her the night before, believing Rachel was staying with me, with *her*, and Faye had had to tell her we were both in Paris, and she didn't know exactly where.

'You have made me look very reckless and foolish, Samantha,' she said. 'This was very stupid.' My head was trying to process it all. I honestly hadn't thought I was doing anything wrong, and I didn't fully understand why Rachel wouldn't have told Madame Lacasse the truth. Maybe the Lacasses weren't as easy going as I'd thought, maybe Rachel had been told she wasn't allowed to go – after all, Victoire hadn't gone, something I'd thought was weird at the time.

'I didn't know Rachel had said that,' I said, telling the truth, because I couldn't think of anything else. 'Everything I told you was true. I told you who we were staying with, and that's who we stayed with. I'm sorry Madame Lacasse didn't know, but I didn't know she didn't know.'

Madame Faye wasn't happy with this. She went off on another rant about how this time I'd gone too far and she was going to have to call my mum.

'But I told you everything,' I said.

'If you told me everything,' Faye said, 'why did your friend tell Madame Lacasse something else?' If I said what I thought, that Rachel just hadn't been allowed to go, then Faye would ask me what sort of party it was, and I'd probably end up in more trouble.

So I just said, 'I'm sorry there was a misunderstanding. I've tried to be truthful. We spent the day in Paris alone together, then we stayed the night with friends; we were safe. They had a party, but we didn't go to any bars, or take the Métro after dark, or put ourselves in any danger.'

'This is your last warning, Samantha,' Madame Faye said. 'I did not agree to have wild English girls who tell me lies staying for the summer. I am *very* disappointed.' There was no point repeating what I'd already said. I went upstairs and called Rachel.

Rachel answered, and simply said, 'I can't talk now,' and hung up. She sounded terrible.

I went downstairs. 'Do you mind if I go out?' I asked Madame Faye. 'I just need to go for a walk.'

'Yes, you can go,' Madame Faye said. 'Be back for dinner.'

I walked straight across one of the corn fields, trying to stamp down as much corn as I could. Crowds of butterflies were disturbed and flew up, and I swatted them aside. Even spotting a tiny rabbit didn't make me stop and go, 'Ahhh, little rabbit!' the way I normally would have – I was too upset and angry. I texted Bruno as I walked, hoping he'd come and meet me in 'our' café and I'd have someone to talk to with soft eyes and a warm smile, who'd just let me be myself and didn't have any reason to let me down or tell me off. He didn't reply, but I went to the café anyway, ordered a big glass of

Coke, and sat there feeling sweaty and sick. By now I was so tired that I physically couldn't eat, and I let my eyes close and felt my head swinging in circles as I fell asleep at the table.

'Hey, wake up – you'll get your bag stolen again.' I jumped, and found myself looking into Bruno's eyes. He was standing close to me with his head tilted to one side, smiling a half smile. Then he frowned slightly. 'Do you have a problem?'

'I just hoped you'd feel like a chat,' I said. 'I don't seem to be friends with anyone else at the moment. Everyone's hating me.'

'Not everyone, I'm sure,' Bruno said, and sat down. I started telling him about Paris, and he was listening, asking questions, being polite, but . . . well, that was the problem. I got the feeling he was *acting polite*, and I'd never felt that way with him before. Like he was bored with me, or was secretly finding me annoying. I couldn't tell for sure if the tiredness and stress with Rachel was just making me paranoid, and I tried to catch his eye and hold it, hoping to find some confirmation that I was imagining his sudden coolness towards me. But he wouldn't even look me in the eye most of the time, and when he did, I had the feeling he was angry about something. He seemed so far away. I was too scared to ask what the problem was, if anything. He sipped his cup of coffee and squinted into the sunshine, looking around the square at other people.

Finally, I said, 'Listen, I really dragged you over here for no reason. I'm sure you didn't want to listen to some long, boring story about English girls in Paris, and I don't have anything else to talk about.'

I hoped he'd reassure me. I hoped this prickly apology would make him realise that I'd noticed his behaviour had changed, and that he'd snap out of whatever funk he was in and loosen up!

That didn't happen.

Instead, Bruno carried on being *polite*, but not really sounding interested ever, and after not much time had passed, he said he had to leave for his sister's rehearsal for the Fouenne festival. This time, I didn't feel confident enough to tease him about it the way I had when we'd last spoken. I felt an urge to say 'Can I come?', but I was so scared of saying it that my heart started pumping in a silly, fast way, even though I knew I wouldn't say it. It was as though a pane of glass had been lowered between us, and I could still see him, but I wouldn't have been able to touch him if I'd wanted, and everything I was saying to him was muffled, so he couldn't hear. I'd missed my chance with him. Blimey, now I knew I'd *wanted* a chance with him! Typical of me to want a boy I couldn't have, but this time I really felt I'd lost something.

Rachel phoned the next morning, and she sounded fine

again. She told me Madame Lacasse had given her a serious talk, but not made that much of it, and she was sorry my Frenchwoman had given me the full works for something that was *her* fault. Finding out Rachel had got off lightly when I was getting a formal warning to be sent home in disgrace *was* incredibly annoying. Seriously, what was up with *my* luck since I stepped out the other side of the Channel Tunnel? Everything worked out for Rachel, everything was hard for me.

'So listen,' Rachel said. 'You know Victoire is having a birthday party the day after tomorrow? You're coming, aren't you?'

She said it as if she'd talked about it before, but it was the first time I'd heard her mention it.

Also, was she bloody kidding? The last thing I wanted was to go to another party. I had to stop myself from yelling at her, Oh yeah, I had such a great time at that last party, eh! But stupidly, I hadn't really managed to shake the feeling that I was to blame for not having as good a summer as Rachel, and part of me wanted another chance.

'Well – am I invited?'

'Yeah of course! It's going to be enormous. Bring Lucas's sister, and then they'll have to give you a lift home.'

'She doesn't really get on with Victoire's circle, though, does she? Are you sure she'd be invited?'

'This place is incredible. Make her come with you.'

I wasn't really comfortable with Rachel asking both of us to a birthday party that she wasn't personally having. I said I'd think about it. These days, every time she talked, Rachel had a slight craziness to her, as if she was trying to make up for the last thing that had happened, and throwing herself into it with fake enthusiasm. She might have been having all the good luck on this holiday, but I was worried she was changing so fast that she was forgetting how to be herself. I decided to ask Chantal about the party. If she wanted to go, I'd go.

Chapter 15

'*Non.* No thank you.' Chantal even started giggling. 'Really, Samantha, does it sound like my sort of party? Lucas maybe. Can you see me putting on a pink dress and dancing to Christina Aguilera at this party with all the girls who ignore me at school?'

I smiled, despite myself. 'You don't have to dance. You don't *even* have to wear a pink dress!' I understood, though. 'You don't have to go. I'm sorry. It just sounds exciting, and I haven't seen Victoire's house, and I thought you might be interested.'

'Will my mother let you go alone?' Chantal asked. 'I'm sorry if I'm stopping you from going. But I really don't have a choice. I have a rehearsal with the band.'

Of course: the totally mad Fouenne medieval festival was a week away. I had spent quite a lot of time thinking about Bruno over the last couple of days, and it occurred to me that if I skipped the party and pretended to be interested in Chantal's band, then I would get to be involved in the festival and run into him casually, like an insider, and we could just start talking again naturally . . . but let's face it, it was wrong of me to try to use Chantal that way. Or could I . . .?

'Oh, how have band rehearsals been?' I said. 'I'd be quite interested in seeing how that's going for you.' *Shameless.*

'You can come along if you like,' Chantal said. 'I thought you might think it was boring. We just repeat the same few songs over and over and over.'

She was right. Was I really up for an evening of that just on the off chance that it would force another meeting with a boy who clearly wasn't into me any more, if he ever had been? Well . . .

I phoned Rachel to tell her there was no way I could go to Victoire's party because I'd have to come alone, it was too far, I had no way of getting home, and now was not the time to take liberties with Madame Faye's mood with me. (Thanks to *you*, I thought, but didn't say it.)

'You know that Lucas is coming, though?' Rachel said. 'Why can't you get a lift home with him? There's no way he's going all the way home to Paris after a party here.'

'How do you know he's coming?'

'Victoire said. Apparently he always goes.'

'But he's mostly in Paris now.'

'He's home often enough. Victoire seems to think he's coming. I told her you'd snogged him.'

'WHAT? Why would you tell her that?'

'I don't know. Just talking, I suppose.'

'But you don't . . . tell . . .' I trailed off. But you're MY BEST FRIEND, I was thinking, and I didn't say you could tell people.

'What is the deal with you and Lucas, anyway?' Rachel said, basically ignoring my frustration about her telling *everyone everything*.

'I don't know,' I said truthfully. 'I thought I *really* fancied him, and then I snogged him and I still thought I fancied him, but then somewhere along the way I just changed my mind. I just sort of chickened out of the whole idea.'

'But he's gorgeous, you know? Everyone I know fancies him.'

An image of Bruno popped up in my head.

Do you know what my problem is? I DO NOT KNOW WHAT I WANT. *Ever.* I want everything at the same time, and to not have to make any decisions. Maybe I *did* still fancy Lucas. Maybe I should go to the party with Lucas, the party I was actually invited to, rather than spend another deadly-boring evening at band practice as part of a complicated plan to chase after Bruno with no chance of success. We were halfway into our summer here, maybe now was the time for me to bring back the old me, the snoggy, party-going me. The fun me. And I *needed* to see the Lacasse house.

'Well, how am I going to get there?' I said.

'Will *no one* give you a lift?' Rachel groaned. 'Call Lucas, ask him to pick you up when he gets here, and bring you.'

'I can't call Lucas.'

'You snogged him and you can't call him?'

'Exactly!'

'When did you become so shy?' Rachel asked.

'When did you stop?' I said.

We were silent.

'OK, I'm going to try to sort this,' she said, and hung up. She called back a few minutes later and said, 'Victoire called Lucas, he's going to pick you up.'

'Noooo!'

'What? We've sorted it out for you. You have to come now.'

I agreed to this, Lucas agreed to this, Chantal completely understood my sudden withdrawal from the band practice (and was maybe just a bit relieved) and, most unexpectedly of all, Madame Faye was fine with it. So Saturday night found me in the kind of pink dress that Chantal made fun of (well, it wasn't really pink, it was dark burgundy with a fitted top half, cut straight across with burgundy straps, but edged with pink ribbon, and a wide pink bow around the waist) waiting for Lucas to turn up on his moped. Chantal had already left, so I waited with her parents, and you can imagine what fun that was. By the time he arrived, I was so relieved to see him that I greeted him with a silly, wide smile. He told his mum he'd get me back before midnight, and we set off. Ack, I'd forgotten about helmet head, and I'd spent so long on my hair!

I don't know what I'd been expecting the Lacasse house to be like, but it was more spectacular than that. It was an enormous farmhouse, ten bedrooms, according to Rachel, with six sets of glass double-doors at the front, some of which were thrown open for the party. Lucas parked his bike in the gravel car park, and we walked towards the house together, unintentionally keeping time with the music we could hear. My hand sort of prickled to hold his, just because I was nervous and he was there, but I held back.

'Wow,' I whispered. 'It's gorgeous.'

'It's a nice house,' Lucas said. He looked down at me and smiled. 'Victoire's a nice girl.' We walked round to the back, from where people's voices could be heard over the music. There were groups of girls in full-skirted prom dresses in a rainbow of colours talking to cute boys in bashed-up jeans. One or two of them looked at us, but it wasn't like making an entrance or anything, people were just milling around outside. I couldn't see Victoire or Rachel. The garden – which went on for miles – was lit with candles in glass jars, around the terracotta paving stones, and amongst the dark bushy trees. It was so beautiful I gasped.

I found Marthe first, who I rushed over to, still feeling grateful to her after the rough night in Paris, although it was really her older sister who'd helped me out. Marthe said she'd just seen Victoire and Rachel in the kitchen, and Lucas stayed outside talking to Marthe while I went in to find them.

The kitchen was gigantic, a lot bigger than our living room at home, complete with a long, rustic wooden dining table and French dressers, and a lovely blue-grey cat in the corner, sleeping through the loud music. Rachel was wearing a dress I'd never seen before, made of soft blue cotton with white lacy embroidery. Her honey-coloured hair was tied in a loose pony tail that fell on one shoulder, her curves were like something out of a cartoon – hourglass figure with a tiny waist – and she was so stunning I could hardly stop looking at her. This was my shy best friend, who had never been out with anyone in England (apart from Ginger Brian). Next to her, Victoire, who was elegantly curveless, looked like a French film starlet. I wondered if there was still time for me to get to the medieval festival band practice with the geeks, where I obviously *really* belonged. My dress, which had once been my ultimate pulling dress, now seemed old-fashioned, and I was embarrassed that I'd worn it so many times.

'Did Lucas bring you?' Victoire asked, while pouring me a glass of Perrier. I nodded, and she looked pleased. 'But his sister didn't come?' When I said no, Victoire didn't seem very interested.

'Let's go out and find him,' she said, taking hold of Rachel's hand. I followed them, and when we were outside, I was shocked to see Bruno talking to a *ridiculously* pretty – was no one at this party *average-looking*? – girl with shiny dark ringlets. I stared for a moment before I realised my mouth had fallen open. I'd worked out what had happened: when I made him come out to meet me in Vernon the last time, he'd already met this girl, and was just being kind to me, but had been bored and uncomfortable, hadn't wanted to be there, had wanted to get away as quickly as he could – that explained his indifference, and the slight air of irritation that had almost seemed at the time like anger. I felt stupid for having bothered him. I had to get away this time before he saw me, or caught me gawping at him. I strode quickly round the side of the house, pushing through a gap in a hedge where the branches of trees crossed over making a kind of leafy doorway, and found a sort of secret courtyard. The gardens around the house were really endless – there were little alcoves and patios and quiet places around every corner. I leaned against the wall for a moment in my old dress, and wondered why I always felt so alone these days. Then I realised I wasn't.

'Ah, I've found you,' Lucas said.

Chapter 16

'Victoire's looking for you,' I said.

'Yes, I've seen her already,' Lucas said. 'With your English friend.'

'Yeah,' I said. 'Oh, thanks for bringing me, by the way. It's an amazing party.'

'It's always the best party of the summer,' Lucas said. Wow, this conversation was both awkward *and* boring. There was a silence, and Lucas broke it by asking, 'What did I do wrong?' His voice was soft and serious.

'I . . . what do you mean?' I asked.

'It was Château-Gaillard, wasn't it?' Lucas said. 'I came at you too quickly. I scared you away. But you seemed to like me then.'

'Well, um, *obviously*,' I said, embarrassed. 'I just . . . it wasn't that you scared me away, I just thought it was a mad idea. I'm staying with your parents, your mum is not exactly happy with the way I've been behaving since I got here, you come home at least once a week, it wasn't very sensible of me to . . .'

Lucas had moved closer, and was touching my wrist with his fingertips, then my hip. I glanced down. What should I do, move his hand? Move myself? 'You can't always be sensible,' he said.

'I think it's . . . it's . . . it's . . .' I couldn't think straight! 'It's always best to try!' I finished brightly. With Lucas easing in closer all the time, I felt a bit like one of those cartoon cats that's been accidentally painted with a white stripe and is being chased by the French cartoon skunk. But he was very, very good-looking, and I knew he was a great kisser, and there was something about being cornered against a wall by Lucas that made me forget common sense and just think about his soft lips. As long as I didn't look at them, I'd be fine.

'That's why you changed your mind, then?' Lucas asked. His fingers were still on my hip, and with his other hand he leaned on the wall behind me. I shivered a little. I looked at his lips. I tried to be sensible.

So there I was, tumbling head first into a long dizzy kiss with Lucas when, totally unexpectedly, I just mentally snapped out of it. His tongue was, at this point, in my mouth, and I realised that not only was I not enjoying it, but I was completely in control of my head and knew this was a pretty disgusting thing to be doing, like asking for a second helping of tough old

Faye family fish. Not because Lucas wasn't sexy – he definitely was, and he'd been really sweet to me, too. But I fancied someone else. And even if they didn't want to know, snogging someone else was immature and . . . well, a bit *slutty*, really. Plus it wasn't fair to Lucas. I pushed him away, gently.

'Lucas,' I said. 'This isn't a good idea.'

'Your body is telling me it's a very good idea,' Lucas murmured, kissing my face. Um . . . yuk?

This is awful, but I was thinking just one thing at this point: if I upset him, how am I going to get home? Then again, given that this palace had *ten bedrooms* couldn't my oldest best friend just let me sleep on the floor of hers? 'I have to go,' I said to Lucas. 'I'm sorry.'

'Why don't you make your mind up?' Lucas snapped, his voice sounding suddenly harder. 'You're being quite a tease, you know?'

Now, back in the days when I used to understand the world, and my friend Rachel didn't have sex with boys who had girlfriends, or stay up all night at parties getting off with complete strangers, some boys at school had accused her of being a tease, and it really made me mad. I used to get really fighty when she reported it back to me. I told her that it was their egos talking. I said they had their chance to make her fancy them, and if they failed, that was *their* fault, and NOTHING to do with any encouragement from her. I told her she could change her mind at any time. I meant it, and I was right. So why, now, when I heard the feeblest, oldest line of the sulking male, was I so upset and deflated by it? Why did it make me feel guilty and stupid and wrong?

I think when you feel confident you can laugh anything off. But when you feel sort of ugly, uncertain, rejected and lovesick, then you believe whatever people tell you about yourself, especially when it's bad. You even feel you've got less of a right to make decisions, and that other people probably have a right to tell you off if you make one they don't like. So, despite knowing better, I just quietly excused myself, and left him there in the little courtyard, trying not to look as if I was ready to cry. Although I was.

I had to find Rachel and Victoire and see if I could stay the night. Madame Faye wouldn't be happy, of course, and would assume I was up to no good. I saw Bruno again, still sitting with the very pretty girl, and our eyes met, but I didn't stop. I found Marthe, who was making a lot of people laugh with a story that she was telling too quickly for me to understand, and I had to wait to the end, pretending to find it funny, so I could ask her if she'd seen Rachel. She said no, but maybe to try the tables at the front of the house.

There were a couple of twirly iron tables outside, which were now covered in empty glasses, but Rachel wasn't there. I sat down at one of them. A little later,

Bruno came and sat down at the next table, but didn't talk to me or look at me. He just sat there quietly as if he'd come to be alone. I stared at him. He looked straight ahead. Finally, I couldn't stand the silence any more, and pushed my chair back, making a scraping sound, determined to say something.

'How are things?' Bruno said, in little more than a whisper, still gazing ahead.

'Oh, I . . .' I said, surprised. 'Things are OK.' I heard my voice crack and wished I could control it better.

'You looked upset. Just now in the garden.'

'No, I was . . .' Well, what was I? 'No, I'm all right.'

'That's good,' Bruno said, turning to look at me for a moment. I shivered. Then he looked down. 'Did you fight with Lucas?'

'I suppose so. No, it wasn't a fight.' I wanted to explain, but I knew that wouldn't be very stylish of me, telling him about a snog with another boy. But Bruno had started off as my friend, even if I'd ended up wanting more from him. The part of me that remembered him as a friend wished I could loosen up and share some of my sadness with him.

'OK,' he said. For some reason I couldn't guess at, he sounded about as miserable as me. 'How are you going to get home? Are you staying here?'

I felt sorry for myself again, and my eyes filled with tears. 'Yes,' I said tightly, trying to sound normal.

'I could do either. I haven't even decided – it's not going to be a problem, though.'

'That's good.' He moved his chair as if he was about to get up. I didn't want him to go, but I didn't want to look desperate, so I thought maybe I'd better go, then he wouldn't think I was bothering him. I opened and shut my little clutch bag.

'Well, I should really find Rachel and see what's happening,' I said.

'Yes, of course,' Bruno said, then in a quite unexpectedly cheerful voice, 'So how are you enjoying your summer?'

I wanted to smile, it was so much a polite, your-friend's-dad sort of question. I appreciated him keeping our chat going on longer, though. I wondered whether to give him the answer you give your friend's dad, or open up, be honest. I went for the latter. 'I think Rachel is having the perfect summer. It's an amazingly beautiful part of the world, and I love being here, and the Fayes have taken me to lots of interesting places, but I don't really feel like I've made it home the way she has. She's just melted into the place and I still feel a lot like an outsider.'

'It's your first time away from home, though?'

I nodded.

'And your friend is staying in a house it's very easy to melt into, *n'est-ce pas*?'

'*Oh, oui, bien sûr,*' I said, laughing at my useless French, and the fact that I still let everyone speak English to me, despite the fact that my mum had let me come here with the understanding that I'd do the opposite.

'If you wanted a change of scene, I was going to take the train to Étretat in a day or two, it's a . . . beach town, but not so much for tourism. Very pleasant for sketching, you know? Would you like me to take you? *As friends,* I mean, of course.'

I'd been getting gradually more hopeful as he made his sketching suggestion, but the carefully added 'as friends' brought me down to earth with a bump. I glanced at him and couldn't help shivering again.

'You look cold,' Bruno said. 'Perhaps you brought a warm coat?' He was wearing a grey jumper over his white T-shirt and he tugged at it. 'Would you like to wear my pullover?'

'Oh no, I've got a cardigan,' I said. 'I left it with . . .' Lordy, I'd left it with Lucas in the little courtyard. 'I'll go and get it.'

I got up clumsily and walked round the house to where I'd left Lucas, hoping he wouldn't still be there, hanging out menacingly to call me a tease. But Lucas *was* there, with some girl. Snogging her face off! I backed away immediately, the way you do when you interrupt people snogging, but a millisecond later my brain processed what I'd seen, and I whirled around again to see that it was RACHEL snogging Lucas. For a moment I couldn't move and just stood there, my jaw hanging, feeling like I'd had a bucket of boiling hot water thrown in my face. I could see my cardigan on a little stone wall and didn't know whether to interrupt them or not, to let them know I could see them. I was so angry I just went for it. I charged over to the cardi, said, 'Excuse me, I left this,' and then clomped away noisily.

But my confidence completely vanished as soon as I was out of their sight. I couldn't get a lift back with Lucas now. There was NO WAY I was asking Rachel if I could stay with her. What was *up* with her? Was she going to snog every boy she met? And fine, I didn't want Lucas any more, but she didn't know that. As friends, she should have made sure I had officially signed off on him, no matter how much I'd hinted at it, before going ahead and snogging him. There are rules! You get permission! I wanted to turn around and go back and say to her, 'You know what? All those years being my saddo friend who never got kissed have meant you've never learned the etiquette of snogging your best friend's ex-snogs,', but I knew that was stupidly mean, and the truth was, I was just jealous of her and felt I'd lost yet again. Sexy mystery-boy Lucas, who all her French friends liked, had been the only thing I had that she hadn't got here. Now even he was hers.

Chapter 17

Good old Marthe, again, gave me a lift in her car back to the Fayes. I talked a little about Rachel, without giving much away, and Marthe told me that Victoire's mum still wasn't happy with her going to Paris without telling anyone, and that they were all a bit disappointed with her. She stayed out late in Vernon quite a lot, sometimes just with boys, when the girls had already gone. It was bizarre hearing people talk this way about Rachel. Marthe said she was going back to the party, and I thanked her for being so nice. I went straight to bed and didn't come out of my room the next morning until I heard Lucas's bike growling down the drive and away, and I knew he'd gone again.

When I started making breakfast, Madame Faye walked in and observed sarcastically that I was beginning my day late. I just wanted to tell her to sod off. She had no idea what had happened and how long

I'd been awake. I looked moodily into my coffee cup. Chantal came in looking sunny and bouncy (in a small gothy way) and asked how the party had gone.

'I didn't have a great time,' I said. 'I wish I'd come out with you instead.'

'Well, you're welcome to come along next time,' Chantal said. 'I don't know if it is your style, though.' We both smiled. 'I didn't speak to Lucas this morning,' she added. She looked at me, as if I might fill in the blanks. I wasn't about to do that.

I was sulking and walking in the fields near the Faye cottage when Rachel called. I'd been imagining the things I'd say to her when we next met, whispering the witty comebacks as I walked. I must have looked insane. When Rachel apologised for snogging Lucas, I was going to stay cool, and act as if I barely even knew what she was talking about. I'd laugh lightly and say something like 'Oh him, who cares what Lucas does, he's just a male tart. *You* should be careful though.'

'Can we talk?' Rachel said. 'Do you fancy meeting in Vernon in the café?'

'What do we need to talk about?' I said coldly.

'Sam,' Rachel said. 'Come on.'

'Well, why don't you come here if you want to talk?' I said.

'I just thought you liked that café.'

'Yeah, it's just always me that has to come and see you,' I said.

'Fine, I'll come and see you,' Rachel said.

'Fine.'

'OK, um, how do I get there, again?'

'I'll come into Vernon,' I sighed. 'Now?'

'Yes, please, now,' Rachel said. 'If you can. As soon as you can.'

We sat there, two best friends, on the holiday of our lifetime, sipping iced tea in a French café.

'I can just tell you're mad at me,' Rachel said.

Wow, really, you think? 'I'm not mad at you.'

'Everything I've done since we got here has annoyed you. You even seemed annoyed at me over Fabrice, when I've never needed you to support me more.' Her voice sounded croaky, and I did feel a pang of guilt.

'You're not you!' I said. 'You haven't been you since we got here.'

'Who am I, then?'

I shrugged.

'Is this about Lucas?' she said.

'Why would it be about Lucas?'

'You saw me snogging him. You obviously still like him.'

'I *don't* still like him,' I said.

133

'Oh, right, I see. Excuse me for thinking there was a problem! If you *don't* like him there obviously can't be one! Why would you be mad at me for snogging someone you *don't* like?'

'Because you don't know I don't like him!'

'So it wasn't you who told me he said you were a little girl and you never wanted to see him again.'

'But you didn't know how I felt about him!'

'I just assumed you were telling me the truth!' Rachel said.

'I was,' I said quietly.

I knew that I could say something nice, meet her halfway, and this would all be over and we'd be friends again. There are moments in life when you can see really easily what's going to happen – every outcome of every action – before you do anything, and before you make the choice you actually have some control. It doesn't happen a lot. In those moments it's like you're a soap opera character and you've suddenly joined the writing team. But it doesn't make you feel good, because you just have less people to blame when it goes wrong. I knew that I could make everything fine by being easy and light, and laughing about what a mess we'd got into, or what fun we were having – something like that. But I was too angry. I wanted her to know it; I wanted her to feel bad; I wanted the apology that was owed to me.

So I watched myself act like a cow to her – almost

as if I was watching it happen to someone else: the character on that soap opera I was now writing – and knowing that at any time I could stop. But not stopping. I wasn't light or carefree, I was sarcastic and ignored her questions and let the silences go on and on. And then, obviously, Rachel didn't have much choice but to do the same. That's how we left things.

Chapter 18

I thought I would let Bruno forget he'd asked me to the seaside with him. There was a good chance he'd only asked because he felt sorry for me when I looked so miserable at the party. So when my phone rang and his name appeared on the screen I was really happy. I'd been wallowing in depression having not spoken to Rachel since our meeting in the café. I knew Bruno just wanted to be friends, but, as I said before, I needed a friend.

Well, that was the idea. But when I saw him waiting for me at the station, all gorgeous-like-he-didn't-know-it, and shy smiles when he noticed I was there, my heart seemed to lift up into my throat and I knew I'd have to keep pulling it back down all day long.

We took a train to Rouen, then le Havre, then a bus to Étretat, and at every stage Bruno apologised for the journey being so long and said he hoped I'd think it was worth it. He didn't seem to realise that I was happy just to be there with him, trundling along through the beautiful countryside, listening to his low voice and funny, too-perfect English. The rest of my life was messed up, but with Bruno things were simple. There was just today, and no hidden meaning behind his talk, and no chance of me getting it wrong again. I wasn't going to blurt out 'Hey, I fancy you something chronic!', because I knew he didn't feel the same way about me. I was just going to chill, take in the day, forget about my embarrassing non-starter of a romance with Lucas and the stressed out arguments with Rachel.

We arrived at Étretat before noon, and when we got off the bus I could smell the sea. An oven-hot blast of sunny air hit me hard after the air-conditioning on the bus, but I shivered with excitement, the way I had as a little girl when I was taken to the seaside. It was an old-fashioned town, with tight little streets. A car was trying to squeeze down one of these, but a huge seagull had chosen to walk very slowly immediately in front of the car, wiggling its hips like a sassy thing, while the car beeped and tried to get it to move. The driver was getting angrier and beeping more, but didn't dare run over it. Finally, the seagull looked sneeringly over its shoulder at the car, turned and flew up on to the bonnet, where it faced the driver eye to eye, until the driver put on his wipers and it screeched huffily and hopped off. Everyone else on the street had stopped to watch, and Bruno and I were laughing so hard.

I fought the urge to hold hands with him.

I know, I know, not cool: it just felt like the kind of day you should be spending with a boyfriend. I'd promised myself I wasn't going to waste the day wishing for more than friendship, but it was difficult.

Still, for a moment, the view took my mind off thinking about throwing myself at Bruno. We were looking out over a tiny curve of shingled beach, sheltered in the carved-out stone of beautiful white cliffs. At each edge of the curve, there was a craggy fairy-kingdom arch in the cliff face, just wide enough for little boats to sail through. We climbed to the top of one of these arches and sat down on the grass looking out over the sea, which sparkled like twirling disco balls, all the way to the horizon.

'When do you go back home?' Bruno asked. 'Would you like a sandwich?' He'd undone his rucksack and taken out a packed lunch, which had been cooled. He offered me a baguette filled with brie and tomatoes, and I realised I was starving.

I took one off him with a greedy smile. 'Hey, thank you. Um, I've got just over a week, give or take a few days,' I said, taking a bigger bite than I'd intended, and talking with my mouth full. 'Sometimes I think that's forever, other times I panic about how late I've left it to . . .' I stopped talking, thinking about the fabulous plans I'd had for the summer, feeling a bit weepy, and took an even bigger bite of the baguette.

'How late you've left it to do what?'

'Well, learn French for one thing,' I said, trying to swallow quickly. 'That isn't happening so much. But this was our first time away from home together – mine and Rachel's – and I thought it was a big deal and that we'd – this is going to sound lame – really start to grow up. Instead it's made me feel younger and less in control than ever before.'

'That's not very unusual, I think,' Bruno said. He was leaning on one elbow now, elegantly sipping water from a little bottle, while I wolfed down lunch. 'It can be quite intimidating to have to make all your choices all at once. Especially when you've been separated from your friend. At home she is sometimes confident enough for both of you, perhaps?'

My heart sank. I wanted to go, 'NO! I'm the cool one! I'm the one boys like! I'm the one with better clothes: check out my cool flipflops!' – but I realised this would only prove beyond any doubt that I was the one who was a total saddo. I took another bite and swallowed it.

After we'd eaten, Bruno pulled open the other side of his bag and produced a tin of sketching pencils, charcoals, and battered, dog-eared sketch pads, then a crisp new pad, which he gave to me. He put the pencils between us.

'You know, I think I might have misled you,' I said. 'I am actually very crap at this.'

'No one's looking,' Bruno said. 'Just let your pencils float over the paper. Everyone is inspired by Étretat.'

So we just sat there quietly, me watching him while his pencils 'floated' over the paper, and making my own little feathery marks on the furry-smooth brand new page. I was thinking, Well, Sam, you've finally made the swap complete. Rachel is probably somewhere snogging someone, and meanwhile this just about counts as homework and you're having a really good time.

I peeked at Bruno's pad, and was surprised to see that instead of the obvious cliffs and horizon, he'd drawn a little old French lady sitting on a bench near us, who'd taken off her shoes and was stretching out her toes and eating a boiled egg with an expression of perfect contentment.

I looked back at my own wonky landscape. 'Gah, this is hopeless,' I muttered to myself.

'Would you like me to take a look?' Bruno asked.

'Well, um, no, I mean, you can, it's just I . . .'

Bruno leaned into me, his face close to mine. 'You're not a bit hopeless,' he said. 'Would you mind if

I . . .?' He reached over my arm with his pencil and added just a few fast strokes to my page. I was distracted by his closeness, and the soft sometimes-touch as his bare arm bobbed into mine. Unbelievably, now the landscape I'd tried messily to construct seemed to hold together, and looked like a proper drawing; I was even proud of it, because it was still recognisably mine. 'It's good,' he said simply, and flashed me an adorable little smile.

We walked down to the beach, wobbling over the stones, and the surge of romance in the atmosphere became painful, because I knew this was just today, and he didn't feel anything I was feeling. Later he'd go and meet his pretty girlfriend, the one I saw him with at Victoire's party, and tell her that today he took pity on that lonely English girl, the one with the more dazzling friend.

But he hadn't mentioned a girlfriend yet. There could have been a dozen different reasons for this, but one of those reasons might have been . . . that he didn't have a girlfriend. Did I have a chance? Bruno always seemed to come along and rescue me just when I needed it, but I had no way of knowing how he felt about me. Sometimes . . . but other times . . . It was useless. It wasn't that I couldn't trust my instincts any more, it was like my instincts were turning to me and shrugging, going, 'Huh? I don't speak French!'

On the way back to the bus stop, we ran into the gull bully again, standing on another car and squawking bossily into the windscreen. We both cracked up laughing, but when we stopped, I suddenly felt very sad because the day had come full circle and now it was over.

'Is everything OK?' Bruno said.

I couldn't really tell him why I was sad, so I started talking about falling out with Rachel, and how upset it had made me. I didn't go into detail, and just babbled about the way we'd both changed since the holiday began.

'I don't know if it's appropriate to say this,' Bruno said, 'but I have to confess that I saw what you saw at Victoire's party.'

'Rachel kissing Lucas, you mean,' I said.

He nodded. 'I feel I should say something now,' he went on. 'Well, I feel I shouldn't say anything, but also that I should have said something before, but I considered the possibility that it was just . . . big talk? And now I have to tell you because I've started to tell you, but it's not my business, and I . . .' He hit his forehead with the heel of his hand. 'I'm very stupid.'

'OK, I have no idea what you're telling me.' I wanted to smile because he was being so serious, but I was also pretty worried.

Bruno grabbed my wrist in his hand, stopping us

walking, and steered me – almost *pushed* me – against a wall to take us off the pavement while we talked. He looked me dead in the eye and sighed hard before he began. Then he talked very, very quickly. 'Samantha, Lucas has made a bet with his friends – some of his friends are some of my friends – that he will sleep with *les Anglaises*, both of you, before you leave. I'm so sorry. I wish I hadn't told you, but I thought maybe there was still time to let your friend know. And I wish I had told you before it was too late.'

'He's *what*? And what do you mean, "before it's too late"?'

Bruno shrugged and turned away, letting my wrist go and putting his hands in his pockets.

'*C'est un salop,*' he muttered – swearing in French.

'But I don't have . . . I'm not in love with Lucas,' I said. 'There's nothing there. He hasn't hurt me.'

Bruno's eyes searched mine. 'OK,' he said.

'He hasn't won his bet,' I said, looking right back at him with the same intensity.

'This is not something you have to tell me,' Bruno said, then with a small half-laugh added, 'But yes, that's good to know.'

'Well, he didn't tell his friends he had, did he?'

'Yes, I'm afraid he did tell his friends he had.'

I sighed heavily. 'But you believe me?'

'Of course.' He smiled again. 'Of course I do.'

'So, you were right to tell me. I'll give Rachel a call and let her know, and that's . . . that's all there is to it. Thanks.' But how could I tell Rachel? She wasn't speaking to me, I wasn't speaking to her, and if the rest of our stay here was anything to go by, how would I even know if it was too late for her? If I told her, she'd think I was jealous because Lucas had ditched me and gone for her.

As we travelled back towards Vernon, we tried to talk about other things, but it was probably obvious that my mind kept wandering back to Lucas and Rachel the whole time. At the station, Bruno took my hand to shake it, which was very French and very formal and not what I wanted from him – this was a good time to grab hold of me and kiss me, if you asked me – but then he didn't let go for so long, and we looked at each other the whole time. I couldn't work out whether his expression was just friendly concern for a lonely foreigner, or if there was something else there. When it became clear there definitely wasn't going to be any kissing, I made myself walk away, and trudged back to the Fayes through a sunset-dyed corn field.

Chapter 19

After that, there was no word from Bruno, and when I went to the café, he wasn't there. I had to accept that he'd only taken me to the seaside to cheer me up after he'd seen how upset I was at Victoire's. Once again, he'd just come to my rescue at the right time. Finally, I decided that for the rest of the holiday, I would give up on falling in love and having the coolest summer ever . . . and learn to embrace my inner geek. I walked, talked and lived medieval festival activities. I decided it was safest to stick close to Chantal. Yes, she was Lucas's sister, but she had nothing to do with that weird tight-knit Vernon crowd. She and her spoddy goth crew did their own thing, and now I did that thing too. I cut out cardboard flowers and superglued them on to hats, cycled to the music shop in the next village when the bass player needed a new G-string (no, not the underwear, the kind you play notes with), and helped them design their make-up. I couldn't get them to drop the heavy black eyeliner, but I did persuade them to add some colour. After all the hard work, I started feeling like I belonged.

'Can you sing?' Antoine the lead singer asked, when Chantal and I arrived at the last rehearsal before the festival.

'Well . . .'

'That's good enough,' he said. 'We need another backing singer. There should be three.'

'But I don't have anything to wear.'

'You can wear what you want.' He looked down at my T-shirt – soft-lemon-coloured, with a picture of a baby lamb on it. 'Or Chantal can give you something of hers?'

I glanced sceptically at Chantal. She raised an eyebrow and smiled that taking-the-piss smile of hers back at me.

So, early on the morning of the Fouenne festival, I found myself trying on Chantal's loose black T-shirt dress and my own black high-heeled peep-toes, and thinking that the goth look actually wasn't all that bad on me. We got a lift from the lead singer in a little open-backed van so we could go and help set up in the cobbled village square. Chantal and I sat in the back, crushed under props and scenery whenever we turned a corner, and the wind whipped and tangled my hair, and I remembered trundling along the same country roads on Lucas's little moped and winced with embarrassment.

The village was decorated with purple and red bunting and wonky hand-written banners advertising the festival. When the van stopped, the chipboard castle fell off the back and immediately broke in half. We all gasped and there was a shocked silence . . . and then somehow everyone was laughing, and I started laughing with them until I was crying. I leaned against the van and realised that now I'd given up trying, and without even really noticing, I was having a great summer.

We were going to perform the ten-minute show three times in the day; once in the early afternoon for kids – a slightly sillier version – then an early evening slot, and a cheekier, more adult performance – not that I got any of the jokes – sometime around midnight, when the hard-core medieval village festival-goers would be loosened up and merry. The festival organisers had arranged a firework display as the finale. There were seven other groups whose shows rotated with ours. One of them was Bruno's sister's. I could see them setting up on the opposite corner of the square. The pretty, dark-haired girl he'd been talking to at Victoire's birthday party was among them. As Bruno hadn't been in touch since Étretat I was too shy to approach him now. But he'd seen me, and came over.

'You're taking part in the festival, then?' he said.

'Yes, I got the casting call at the last minute,' I said. 'I'm even singing. Although I think they may live to regret that.'

'Oh, I'm sure that won't be the case,' Bruno said, shaking his head. There was a silence which threatened to be awkward. 'I wonder if you'd like to meet my sister, Claudine.' Ah, I thought, the dark-haired girl is his sister! Tra la la!

Except Claudine was a blonde, her hair cut into a half-inch all over crop. We talked about her play – in French, Bruno filling in the gaps for me when I was struggling. She was explaining the plot – it was an old local legend about two doomed lovers who had given the name to a famous valley a few miles away. I asked her if she was playing the lead.

'No, that's Hélene. My girlfriend,' Claudine said, and she waved over at her drama group, and the pretty dark-haired girl waved back!

'That's her?' I said, trying to look like I wasn't shocked. Obviously I wasn't shocked because she had a girlfriend (well, maybe a tiny bit) – it was because she wasn't Bruno's girlfriend!

There was no real time to talk. Our first performance was in a couple of hours, the scenery was being held together with a few lumps of Blu-tak, and I – with no real rehearsals – was going to be standing on stage in front of real people. Yes, it was likely that no one would notice I was there, I could probably get away with miming, and I knew the words because I'd seen it played about a thousand times, but still, I was nervous. The village square, quite empty when we first arrived, was now full of stalls and carts selling toffee apples and crepes, T-shirts and little flags on sticks with a picture of the Fouenne festival mascot – a big, purple cat-like thing – printed on them, and little kids and their parents were starting to arrive to take a look around.

'Good luck,' Bruno said, and squeezed my elbow. I could feel the pressure of his fingers after he'd let go.

'You too,' I said, and hurried back to my gang.

With almost no warning, I went all wobbly with nerves during the first performance. I forgot the words, twirled the opposite way from the other two girls, and shook the whole time I was on stage. This was a little amateur village fête, and I was only standing at the back singing 'ba ba ba baaa' in the chorus, but you'd have thought I was doing a first night gig in front of fifty thousand people. Anyway, the little kids didn't seem to notice I'd got it wrong. Their faces were adorable: they were laughing (mostly when they were supposed to), sucking lollies, clapping and trying to sing along to our punk songs. They seemed to be having a brilliant time.

Despite being petrified, I loved it.

Claudine's play was a lot more talky – I didn't understand it at all – and the only music was played on an old fashioned lute-type thing. Bruno was the narrator, a wandering minstrel, and he came on wearing a kind of all-in-one lycra outfit, and, as he had promised all those weeks ago when he first mentioned the festival, there was dancing. And yet, none of this made him look stupid. For one thing, I couldn't *believe* he had such a great body – his normal day-to-day clothes didn't show his shape as well, and I have to confess my jaw dropped when I saw how fit he really was. The audience loved him, and he was loose and swish as he talked to them, sitting on the edge of the stage with his legs dangling, winking at girls in the audience and making everyone laugh and applaud. And at one point, he found me in the audience and said a line in English looking straight at me, and my heart pounded the way it had when I'd been on stage myself.

Also, I became slightly obsessed with looking at his bum in the lycra outfit.

The next round of performances wasn't for a few hours, and all the performers got some food – the day had flown by and I had barely realised how starving I was – and sat together on stairs outside the church. Bruno had pulled his jeans back on and came and sat next to me.

'You were very good,' he said.

'You too,' I said.

Bruno laughed and blushed. 'It was nice of you to try, but no one believes you,' he said. 'I'm making an idiot of myself. My sister can be very persuasive. Will you be staying for all three performances, or do you have somewhere more exciting to go?'

'More exciting than a medieval festival? Is that possible?' I said, making my eyes pop. 'You know I'm joking, don't you? I can't believe how much fun I'm having. I want to stay all night and do the same thing all over again tomorrow, except this time remember the words and twirl the right way.'

His face crinkled into a gorgeous smile. 'Samantha, you're lovely,' he said, and both of us seemed a little surprised by it, and didn't know what to say next. So we ignored it and pointed out interesting things in the square and watched the festival mascot dance around in his costume defying the summer heat, and I tried not to think too hard because that never got me anywhere.

Chapter 20

After the sun had set, the square seemed to glow with a thrilling new edge of danger, like a fairground. Tons more people had turned up. The tiny little kids had gone, the ones who'd been allowed to stay up were running around with sparklers, the stalls that had been quietly grilling takeaway snacks for everyone all day suddenly looked like blazing furnaces, and the people who milled around were louder and clumsier – I worried about them bumping into our fragile backdrops, which were showing signs of wear and tear after the first two performances. They only had to make it through one more show, and so did I.

We started setting up just after eleven. I saw Victoire first, wearing a white strapless dress and looking like a goddess. Then Rachel and Lucas followed, holding hands and laughing, Rachel leaning against his shoulder and stumbling a little in her heels.

I felt sick. I didn't want them here. Immediately, I was on the defensive, my mind running anxiously through all the reasons our show was stupid and lame, and I thought about not going on. I was angry with her and frightened of her, but I owed her one more thing.

Lucas.

I hadn't told her that the boy she was here with had made a bet about being able to sleep with her, or that he'd lied about having slept with me. She was my best friend and she needed to know. OK, maybe since making the bet he'd fallen head over heels for her, maybe he'd even confessed and they'd both had a big fat laugh about me together. You know how when you start imagining something that *might* have happened, you start believing it *has* happened – and just thinking about this possibility made me hot and angry again. She suddenly saw me and we stared at each other across the square, and in that one moment I wanted to tell her about Lucas to *hurt* her, not to protect her. The feeling was gone a second later, but still.

Our final performance was due to start in less than half an hour. The 'cool' Vernon crowd – about ten of them, now – were wandering around the square together, buying cups of hot apple punch and shouting jokey questions at the mascot, who was now relaxing with his cat-head off. During the first play they began to get quite rowdy, and were shushed by the rest of the crowd. I was dreading going on and wondered if I should just run away now. But Lucas wouldn't let them shout things when his sister's band was playing, would he?

What probably saved us was the volume of our music: it was near-deafening . . . and we rocked it. I could see a few of Victoire's male friends making fun of our dancing, but I didn't care. It just made me dance more crazily myself; I really threw myself into it, tossed my hair around, had a fab time. When we'd finished and the audience applauded like mad, we did a big group hug, and then bowed in a line, holding hands. I didn't want to leave the stage. I wished we could start again from the beginning and go on playing all night.

Bruno's play was next up, but they didn't have a stack of amps, just a lute. Needless to say, the heckling got worse, and when Bruno came out in his lycra bodysuit they wolf-whistled and laughed and shouted things. Claudine was looking close to tears, and I was worried about her.

Bruno looked angrier and angrier, but it was when Lucas shouted in English – I'm not sure why, maybe it was to show off to Rachel – 'Hey, pussy cat! Pooossy cat!' as Bruno was dancing, that Bruno appeared to lose it. I could see him flush very red, and prayed he'd just go on and ignore it. But his hands were balled into tight fists, and as the taunts got louder he suddenly lurched towards Lucas, then stepped back again, glancing at his sister, who seemed to calm him down. The play carried on, and I stopped holding my breath and tried to enjoy it. But when the next song began, my back prickled with fresh sweat, and I scanned the audience nervously. Lucas began calling out again, this time on his own, 'Pooooossy cat!' and making kissing sounds. Bruno's eyes flashed up and stopped on mine and I tried to mouth 'no', but it was no use. He jumped off the stage and punched Lucas in the face. Lucas went down. There was a big crowd gasp, then it all went absolutely silent for a few moments. Then Lucas got up and threw a punch back, which Bruno ducked, and Lucas jumped on him, grabbing him round the neck with one hand, trying to mash his face with the fingers of the other, and then they were totally hard at it, punching each other, and the crowd went mad, half of them shouting at them to stop, the others telling them to go for it. Chantal was screaming at Lucas. Finally one of Claudine's friends and one of Lucas's friends pulled them apart.

They were still shouting at each other, and I could mostly follow their French, although it came very fast. Bruno was accusing Lucas of being the great stud and the great liar, and saying he owed his friends their money back from the bet. Lucas was shouting 'How do you know?' over and over, and his friends started laughing at him and telling him to pay up. Lucas suddenly flew at Bruno again and punched him, knocking him to the ground. Without thinking, I ran over and knelt down next to him. Bruno looked up at me with a dazed expression. You remember that tip I had for making boys want to kiss you, looking at their mouth, then their eyes, then the mouth again, blah blah blah?

Well, you don't always have time for all that. I held his face with one hand and planted my lips on his.

This sounds like I made it up, but I swear it's true: at that exact moment, the firework display started up on the other side of the square – maybe it was to take people's attention away from the fight – and when I opened my eyes again, Bruno was still looking dazed, but smiling, and the air smelled of gunpowder and above us the black sky was glittering with falling stars.

'That was quite a kiss,' Bruno said. I kissed him again.

Lucas had stropped away, having got in the knock-out punch, and Chantal was following him, shouting at him.

Then I looked over and saw Rachel and realised I didn't have anything to tell her any more, because, of course, her French was better than mine. But as I continued to watch her, I noticed her face was blotchy and tight, with that held-together look I knew well, the one she always had when she was just about to cry. All my anger and nastier impulses were gone in a second, and I just wanted to grab her hand and run for it with her, away from France. But she was already going, without me.

I got up and ran after her.

'Rach,' I shouted, but she kept going. I caught up and grabbed the top of her arm.

'What?' she hissed, whirling round to face me. Her eyes were full of uncried tears.

'I was going to tell you about Lucas,' I said. 'I only just found out.'

'Yeah, like you're not loving this.'

'What are you talking about?' Rachel stared at the ground, and started crying. 'Rach,' I said uselessly. 'Don't cry. Please don't.' I tried to hug her, but she didn't accept it, she just stood there, all hard, with stiff arms and shoulders, and I felt stupid and eventually had to let go.

'OK, are we done, then?' Rachel said, with her voice high and whispery.

I didn't say anything. Couldn't. I knew how this would come across, but I wasn't angry. I was humiliated and scared for her; scared for both of us. But I wasn't crying, or even close to crying, and I felt bad about that too. I watched her until she met up with Victoire again, and Victoire gave her a hug which she *did* accept, and then they both looked at me, and I knew I was being talked about. I stopped looking.

I went back to my friends. Chantal looked up at me with dark, angry eyes, and I could tell she thought this had all been about *les Anglaises*, and that she and her friends were pretty sick of us now. God, there was virtually no one in France who didn't hate me now.

Virtually, but not quite no one.

Bruno, who'd been sitting with his sister while she fussed over his cuts and bruises, stood up and came over to me. He lowered his chin and tilted his head on one side to try to see my face.

'Plenty of fireworks tonight,' he said. 'How are *you*?'

'How are you?' I said.

Bruno shook his head. 'It's nothing,' he said. 'You haven't made up with your friend, then?'

'No.'

'It's his fault, all of this. You should both be angry with him, not each other.'

'Yeah, I know,' I said.

He reached out and pulled me to him, kissing my forehead. 'And what are we going to do now?'

'What do you mean?'

'I mean that you're leaving the country in less than a week, and I'm inconveniently falling in love with you.'

Around us and under our feet there were burned

158

out sparklers and half-eaten chicken legs; pink and purple streamers trampled into the dust, and broken plastic cups. The square was emptying. The party was over.

Chapter 21

So you've fallen hard for this boy, but in less than a week you have to separate. You don't know when you'll see him again, but it won't be any time soon. What do you do with that week? Start it or finish it? Walk away now before you begin to care too much or live it up because this may be all there is?

I can tell you what we did. We laughed a lot about the terrible timing. We told each other off for not doing something about it earlier.

'You were, I think, swept off your feet by Lucas,' Bruno teased me, picking a poppy and tucking it behind my ear.

Argh, if only this weren't true!

I blushed as red as the flower and giggled behind my hands. 'Lucas had the guts to kiss me!' I said. 'If I'd waited for you, we'd never have kissed at all!'

'But I protected you from a dangerous street

robber!' Bruno said. 'That's not enough for you? It always seems to work in movies.'

'You told me you just wanted to be friends. That's what I say to boys when I'm dumping them.'

'Oh, you always torture me by telling me about all your other boyfriends,' Bruno said, whirling me on to my back and snogging me. But whenever I opened my eyes again, and sometimes his eyes were still closed and I could just *look* at him for a second or two, his soft lips just-kissed, I thought about the end. I thought about going home without him, and waiting and waiting for his emails and wondering who else had smiled at him that day, and I felt achey and sad. I knew ten thousand girls had holiday romances every summer and I was just a statistic – worse, a cliché. But some people must actually fall really in love, it can't *always* be a spell the sun casts that fades with your tan.

Bruno rolled over and lay on his back next to me, dragging his hand through the long grass.

'I'm not going to look at you when I say this, because I don't want to see your reaction,' he said suddenly. I was propped up on one elbow and I could see his face, his eyes were closed. 'I want us to not let this go. You and me. I know the odds are against us and you may get home and smile with your friends about the boy you met on holiday and feel very differently. But I *am* home. And when you go, I'm going to start

161

doing whatever I have to to get you back.'

Did I really know what he was feeling? Did it matter? The orangey evening sunshine lay on us like a blanket, and I felt fuzzy and safe, as if I had always been there and always would be. I lifted my head to rest it on his chest, and he stroked my back, and I thought that I would never, as long as I lived, regret this time, and how happy I was right now.

When I wasn't with Bruno, my life was, like the brown meat at the Fayes', quite a bit tougher. Word had got to Monsieur and Madame Faye about the fracas at the village festival, and they obviously blamed the foreigners. There were a few sarcastic comments over dinner about the English liking to fight in public, which was a bit rich – it had been their son throwing the punches. And all through the last few days I was totally dreading Lucas coming home for another visit and running into him at the breakfast table, cutting a slice off that horrible cold sausage. Luckily it didn't happen.

Chantal didn't seem to blame me for any of the trouble. I went out with her and the band one last time, and they were all great; we ended up laughing a lot talking about the night of the festival. It felt good to have been part of it, and to have been one of the performers, rather than one of the too-cool-for-school crowd who came along and spoiled the show. I liked that I'd somehow tumbled into doing the kind of thing I would never have done back home – and loved it – and couldn't stop grinning to myself when I thought about the moment when Victoire's friends started making fun of us and we all just went for it and danced like mad. All the same, because I'd been particularly involved in the fighting that ruined the evening, the confidence I'd built up with the band had deserted me. I felt shy and guilty, and mostly kept quiet.

I called Rachel every day for the rest of our holiday, but she didn't answer. I started to get really worried about her and sent her a text saying, *Just tell me you're OK, then I'll leave you alone.* She texted back *I'm OK*, so I had to do what I'd promised. That was the last I heard from her until we met at Vernon station, with our bags. I was there first. I told Madame Faye I didn't need a lift, and I walked there with Bruno, who wanted to take the train to Paris with me. We were sitting on the bench together, not speaking much because we were feeling miserable, and I saw Madame Lacasse zoom past in her super-flash sports car, and a few minutes later there was Rachel, trying to find some place in the tiny station where she wouldn't have to sit with us.

'Hey,' I said.

'Yeah, hey,' Rachel said, but she didn't come over. The three of us got on the train together and Bruno carried on Rachel's rucksack as well as mine, but she still went and sat away from us, and read a book.

'You have to go and talk to her,' Bruno said gently.

'But in a couple of hours I have to leave you. We don't have any time left. Anyway, we talked to her at the station, she doesn't want to talk to me.'

'*Cherie*,' Bruno said. 'She's your friend, she's on her own, and you're here with me, of course she won't approach you. Come on, let's go and sit with her.'

'But it could go wrong. And you'll soon be gone,' I said. I sounded whiny. He squeezed my elbow, and nodded towards her.

The two of us got up and slid into the double seat opposite Rachel's.

'We thought we'd join you,' I said.

We talked in a clumsy way until we got to Paris, as if there was a camera on us that made us self-conscious. No one mentioned the fight, or Lucas. We chatted a bit about Victoire and Chantal, and Bruno and Rachel talked about some of the towns Rachel had visited, and we even laughed a couple of times. Then there was a fumbled, rushed moment when we transferred to the Eurostar check in – I'd thought Bruno would be able to come further but he couldn't, Rachel had already checked through, and I thought I should go with her to build on the progress we'd made on the train to Paris.

Our time was up. We were just standing there not knowing how to leave each other, I didn't think my legs would let me walk away from him. I closed my eyes and leaned on him.

'Don't forget me,' Bruno whispered in my hair.

'Are you crazy?' I choked, worried he was saying that this was it, the last time we'd see each other. He squeezed me harder and kissed me over and over, and then let go.

We sat together, obviously, on pre-booked seats. Rachel slowly and carefully unpacked some French magazines, an apple, a bottle of water and her MP3 player, placing each of them carefully on the table in front of us. I deliberately didn't put anything out, hoping she'd realise this meant I wanted to talk first.

'Rach,' I said. 'I don't know what's going on with us right now, but I hope we get past it.'

'Mm,' she said, stiffly.

I got quite angry. 'Look, for God's sake, maybe you can't stand me right now, but you could at least tell me why. I can't believe you're just going to give me this silent crap.'

'Oh, leave me alone, Sam,' Rachel said, and I realised she was crying. 'You've had your perfect little holiday romance: you win, you're the best. Naturally you want to talk about it all the way home, but if you don't mind, I'm just going to listen to some music and try to sleep.'

'I genuinely don't know what you're talking about,' I said.

Rachel sighed. 'This summer was the first time I wasn't just Sam's saddo friend, the person waiting to hear what happened to Sam tonight. I did my own thing, I had my own stories. And for some reason that really bothered you. For some reason you have to be the only one we talk about and the only one with a life. You know, fine, fair enough, if that's what you need. But forgive me for just this once wanting to take a break from the next chapter of Samantha Barnes's Diary, OK?'

'I just don't know how you can say that, or think that,' I said. 'You didn't just "do your own thing", you had a total personality transplant and you expect me not to *worry* about that even slightly? But every time I tried to find out how you were, you got really angry and said I was judging you.'

'You *were* judging me!'

'Well, why shouldn't I? You kept screwing up!'

'How do you know?' Rachel snapped loudly, and everyone in the carriage looked at us. 'How do you know what I wanted?'

'Yeah, well, it was a really sane idea hanging out with someone who told the whole town he was going

166

to have sex with both of us for a bet! Smart, Rachel!'

'Thanks,' Rachel said in a tiny voice. 'Now, if you don't mind, I'm going to go back to my music.'

'Rach, I'm sorry,' I said.

'No doubt,' Rachel said.

When our parents met us at King's Cross, they were all weepy and huggy and I tried not to let it show that we weren't talking to each other, because I didn't want my mum to ask questions. Luckily, she didn't notice. She gushed all the way home about how much she'd missed me and asked me a million questions, and I closed my eyes and laid my head back on the car seat, and just yawned and said I was glad to be back.

There was an email from Bruno waiting for me when I got in. I was happy and excited and read it twenty times, but the reason I stayed at my computer for so long was because I was hoping Rachel would send something too.

Chapter 22

I was surprised by the shame I felt when word got around that Rach and I weren't friends any more. It was almost like a divorce: we'd been friends from the beginning. I told myself I wouldn't bitch about her or say anything bad about what happened in France, but then I'd hear things she'd been saying about me and . . . well, I was an idiot to think they hadn't been distorted somewhere along the line, but I fell for all of it anyway, and couldn't help coming back with little snide asides. So the line was drawn and the people we knew tended to fall on one side or another.

Team Rachel was certainly more exciting than Team Samantha. Rachel was charm on toast, with her new dress sense, her new way of walking, the confidence and strength. And for what it was worth, the mere fact of her having lost her virginity seemed to give her some kind of membership card to a new club. I don't know how that worked, but the girls who *had*, seemed to share a different closeness; they talked with authority. For the first time, I understood why people felt under pressure to join that club, and not just pressure from boys. I sometimes wondered if I should have taken things to the next stage with Bruno, but I knew that rushing into anything wouldn't have been proof of our feelings, and could have made a good thing tricky. Some people just need a little time; I'm one of those people.

Bruno and I email every day, sometimes a couple of times a day. Sometimes we instant message, sometimes we even phone. When we're just typing, and Bruno is just words on a screen, I sometimes worry that nothing is real – that it's a nice internet friendship, but my memory has played tricks on me and there wasn't a real romance. Then we'll talk on the phone again, and his voice always sounds different at first, but quickly, everything comes back the way it was.

We're meeting in London next month, December the eleventh, after his term finishes. When I try to guess what will happen to us I get scared or excited, and both ways, my heart beats a lot faster. *Que sera sera* – oh, that's almost the same in French.

Speaking of French, yesterday we had a double period of it, and Ruby Garway (who has tried to stay neutral after the big break-up, but I think is a bit more on my side than Rachel's) was presenting her essay on *Boule de Suif*, a French novella, to the class. Our teacher, Ms Mathur, was asking her questions, and as Ruby stuttered through her pre-prepared answers it was as boring as these things usually are. But then Rachel suddenly spoke up and argued with Ms Mathur about what the end meant – I'd explain, but you'd be bored, I'd have to tell you like the whole story and I'd be using French quotes and I don't know how good your French is – and Ms Mathur argued back in her brilliant French, and then I heard my own voice adding to the debate, in strangely fast and fantastic French that I would never have believed I was capable of. I was doing the accent, even, and I'd always felt stupid doing that, especially in England. Rachel answered me, and I answered her – it was the most we'd said to each other in one go since getting off the Eurostar, and you could hear everyone in the class getting all twitchy and excited because it was us, the famous rivals and fall-outs, talking to each other in French, and because our French was suddenly completely ace (compared to the way we'd been before). Then we looked at each other, just for a moment, and Rachel's eyes gleamed and I saw her smile, as if she couldn't help it, and I couldn't help smiling too. Both of us turned our mouths down again as much as we could, but the gleams and the smiles had escaped and there was no real way of fetching them back.

But we walked out of the class still ex-best-mates, and didn't speak again all day. When I got home the first thing I did was check my emails, but there was nothing. I checked again at about ten, and the inbox was bold and black with the promise of an email.

Bruno had written.

His email made me smile, but it didn't compensate for the disappointment, and somewhere inside me, I ached. I immediately started writing an email to Rachel. I kept thinking back to when we were kids and I'd phoned her after she'd seen the cartoon I drew of her in the sweaty tracksuit, and how simple it had been in those days to make someone like you again. In the email, I said that with all my big plans for us to spend our summer together, I'd messed up, and I'd actually made sure we spent it apart. No wonder it'd had been hard for us, we'd never been separated before. I told her this was one of the most important moments of our lives – one of those forks in the road – and we might never get the moment back.

We spent our lives building this friendship,

I wrote,

and we're going to let one summer kill it?

I worked on the email all night, writing and rewriting, and when I thought I'd got it right, I stopped and stared at the send button, the arrow of the mouse trembling above it.

I moved the email to my drafts folder and went to bed.